PRINCE OF CATS

AUTUMN COURT #1 (ROSETHORN VALLEY
FAE ROMANCE)

TASHA BLACK

13TH STORY PRESS

13th Story Press

PO Box 506

Swarthmore, PA 19081

13thStoryPress@gmail.com

TASHA BLACK STARTER LIBRARY

Packed with steamy shifters, mischievous magic, billionaire superheroes, and plenty of HEAT, the Tasha Black Starter Library is the perfect way to dive into Tasha's unique brand of Romance with Bite!

Get your FREE books now at tashablack.com!

PRINCE OF CATS

1

PIPER

Piper Lee looked over at her best friend and laughed.

Allie, usually so serious, was dancing to a Christina Aguilera throwback song, after joyously proclaiming it to be a "real banger." A glass of white wine sloshed in her hand as Allie gave it everything she had, swinging her hips, one arm waving over her head.

"Come on, Piper," Allie yelled to her. "You only live once. Get over here and dance with me."

Piper smiled and shook her head.

"Our lives are about to change," Allie whined. "We might never have another chance."

That was a bit melodramatic.

But Piper surrendered and shimmied over to join her friend. The party at the old Rosethorn Valley mansion was packed. Piper wasn't usually one to dance while anyone was looking, but the ballroom was too crowded for anyone to be paying attention to her.

"That's right," Allie said approvingly, slinging an arm over Piper's shoulder. "You have to let loose and have some fun once in a while."

"Ladies, what are you drinking?" a guy asked, looking straight at Piper's chest.

"Nothing," Piper said a little too loudly.

He shook his head and slouched along.

"Piper," Allie chided, giving her a little shove.

"I'm not here to get hit on," Piper said lightly. "I thought this was our last chance to hang out for ever and ever?"

She arched an eyebrow at Allie, earning her a hearty laugh.

"Aren't you even a little freaked out?" Allie asked.

Piper knew she should be. She'd spent her whole life dreaming of qualifying for the Olympic archery team. But now that it had actually happened, it mostly felt surreal. The victory at the World Championships had seemed to unfold in slow motion.

She was officially on her way to being an Olympian. And she had a full year to prepare.

Which meant that Allie was right in a way, she wasn't going to be hanging out as much, with Allie, or anyone. She would barely have time to come up for air over the next year. And she could kiss what passed for her social life goodbye.

But she wasn't the only one with a reason to celebrate.

"You know I've planned for this for a long time. I'm happy but I'm not freaked out," Piper said, wishing it was completely true. "But this party is about *you*. You're the one who just finished nursing school. And now you're going to be the best NICU nurse ever."

"That's right," Allie said, eyes shining. "It's going to be hard work, but I'll be holding babies for a living."

"Not a bad gig," Piper agreed.

Another guy approached them.

"No thank you," Piper said before he could even open his mouth. "We're kind of having a moment here."

"Sheesh, Piper," Allie said. "You ever think *I* might like to get hit on tonight?"

"No," Piper said. "If you wanted that, you wouldn't be dancing with me."

Allie rolled her eyes. But when another favorite song came on, she squealed with delight and they danced on. Piper wondered if her friend had any songs that weren't her favorite.

Piper looked around the mansion as they moved to the beat.

When Allie had suggested renting it for the party, Piper had thought she was crazy. Who decided to have a big house party at a stuffy old mansion?

But the ballroom was well suited to the crowd. The black and white marble floors and the huge mirror were so ancient they felt almost ironic against the backdrop of jeans-clad dancers. She felt like she was in a music video.

The weather was perfect, and dozens of people had moved outside through the open doors, crowding the patio surrounding the koi pond. The party even spilled out into the rose garden below.

A flash of movement in the mirror caught her eye and she tried to focus on it, but it was gone.

Piper shook her head.

Of course there's movement in the mirror, she told herself. *There are like fifty people dancing in front of it.*

But that was just it. Whatever she'd seen, it had caught her eye because it hadn't moved like a human at all.

She chalked it up to just being tired. It had been a long day already after getting up to practice at dawn. And she was going to be up early to practice again tomorrow.

Hang out for a little longer, she told herself. *Allie will be sad if you don't celebrate with her.*

But then she spotted the movement in the mirror again, and actually got a decent look at it this time.

It looked like a cat, but it was huge, with glowing, yellow eyes.

As she watched, its reflection disappeared into the dark hallway behind her.

She spun around and craned her neck, trying to get a better view down the real hallway.

But there was no trace of it.

"You okay?" Allie asked.

"Yeah, I've got to go the bathroom," Piper said distractedly.

"Sure," Allie said. "Bring me a drink when you come back?"

"Sure," Piper agreed.

She moved through the other dancers, barely avoiding the hips and elbows circling wildly in time with the music, until she reached the hall and broke away from the crowd.

Compared with the ballroom, it was almost unnaturally quiet in the corridor. The thick old walls must be great at blocking sound. She'd only gone halfway down, but the party already sounded far away.

A whisper of movement near the back of the hall got her attention, and she jogged a little to catch up.

It was definitely some kind of animal. She could just make out the soft fur sliding over sinuous muscle in the soft light.

It had a feline kind of movement, but was far too big to be a house cat. She knew that it wasn't a great idea to go chasing after some kind of wild animal, but she couldn't seem to help herself. It was like the thing was calling to her, even though that didn't make any sense.

The creature turned a corner and Piper dashed after it.

But when she stepped into the adjoining corridor, she came up short.

There was no sign of the cat.

Only a man, leaning against the wall, gazing at her intently, almost as if he'd been expecting her.

He was tall and lean, his muscular frame evident under leather breeches and a silky white shirt. One black leather boot rested on the floor, the other was braced against the wall. On anyone else, the outfit might have seemed odd or out of place, but it suited him perfectly.

"Hello, my love," the stranger said in a lazy, honeyed timbre.

Something about his voice tickled her insides. Piper found herself unable to reply.

He chuckled, and the flash of his smile made her forget to breathe for a moment.

"I saw you in the mirror," he said simply. "Walk with me."

She'd never met this man before. She had no idea who he was, or what he wanted. But when he took her hand, she found she had no desire to shake it off. Instead, a rush of warm fuzzy tingles washed over her.

Piper gasped.

She had done her share of dating. But she had never felt that *zing* they talked about in the romance novels she binged on. She had never felt like she was losing herself over someone.

She'd been into guys before, but this feeling was something altogether different. It made anything she'd thought of as attraction feel like listening to music through a passing car window, compared to sitting front row for the live orchestra.

"Don't be frightened," the man murmured. "Come with me."

But she wasn't frightened. Even though her mind told her maybe she should be.

Piper had spent her whole life making measured choices, being disciplined and practical.

But in an instant, this man had made her feel she would be willing to try anything. She would let him buy her a drink, go drag racing, maybe even jump off a cliff if he told her it would be okay. Anything that would make this heat in her blood and lightness in her heart continue for one more second.

She was addicted, she knew that much, and he hadn't even told her his name.

2

PIPER

Piper allowed herself to be coaxed up the curving staircase.

"I am Killian," the man murmured, as if he had read her mind. "I'm going to show you pleasure you cannot imagine."

His words seemed to shimmer in the air before entering her ears. Was he even speaking out loud?

She wasn't sure. She didn't care.

They walked on, passing room after room.

At last he threw open a thick walnut door at the end of the upstairs hallway.

Moonlight from the big windows illuminated a canopied bed.

There was nothing else in the room.

He drew her to the window, and she gazed out over the circular driveway and the woods beyond as he held her from behind, looking over her shoulder.

"So beautiful," he murmured, that confident voice filled with wonder.

She thought he was talking about the view, but he

pulled her hair away from her neck and lowered his face to nuzzle the tender flesh, sending a shiver down her spine.

"Mine," he growled, his voice half-strangled.

She felt him tugging at her clothing and she helped him, turning lifting her arms, allowing him to undress her as if she were a child. Losing herself in the moment.

He led her to the bed, and she lay down, trembling, wondering what had come over her, if she was really going to allow this to continue.

Piper Lee didn't do one-night stands. She wasn't spontaneous. Piper was a planner.

But how did you plan for this?

The man called Killian stood before her, the breeze from the open window caressing him lovingly, sliding invisible fingers through his long hair, billowing the white shirt so that he looked like a hero right off the cover of one of her romance novels.

Or maybe not the hero...

There was a darkness to him. Something dangerous that clung to him like a fog on a moonlit lake.

She watched as he unbuttoned the shirt, then slid down the leather breeches as he stepped out of the boots.

Piper had always been of the firm opinion that men looked silly naked - pale and helpless.

But somehow, this man managed to look even more powerful without his clothing than with it.

The moonlight highlighted the bulges and planes of muscle, throwing the grooves between them into sharp relief. He stood proudly, allowing her to drink him in.

And then he was moving for her, graceful as a cat.

She held her breath, even her heart seemed to stop beating for a moment.

He pinned her to the bed with his hips, his big body

covering hers. Even the woodsy scent of him permeated her senses until she was consumed with him.

She searched his handsome face. Who was this man?

His eyes glittered dangerously as he studied her as well.

Then he lowered his face to kiss her and she felt like she was flying out of her body, an unearthly longing pounding like a drum in her blood.

She threw her thighs around his hips, clinging to him as if she might be physically borne away by the sensations she felt.

He groaned, dragging his mouth from hers to nip her neck on his way to her breasts.

Piper arched her back, desperate to feel him on her aching nipples.

When he took one in his mouth and flicked his tongue, the pleasure was so intense that she could only moan and tangle her hands in his hair.

He fed on her breasts for a long time, licking and sucking as if he could not get enough of her.

When need twisted her insides so that her hips began to tremble, he moved further still, nudging her thighs apart impatiently to get at her sex.

Piper wailed as he licked and tormented her hungry opening, feasting on her madly without letting her taste relief. He only smiled against her thigh as he continued his relentless assault.

The sensations were like colors flooding her field of vision, fiery scarlets and golden flashes washing over her as she begged for release.

At last, he crawled up to her again and kissed her, his mouth still glistening with the evidence of her desire.

Piper whimpered, unable to form the words to tell him what she needed.

He entered her so slowly she saw stars. He was rigid, and so huge she could barely take him.

He continued, slowly, until at last he was fully seated.

Piper clutched his shoulders and tried to lift her hips, desperate for movement.

He thrust once, slowly, and then again, his rhythm deep and steady.

Piper closed her eyes against the pleasure and saw a mountain of scarlet trees, the footprints of a big cat on a wooded trail, a sparkling river full of shimmering fish, tiny lights dotting the twilight sky.

Killian groaned and sped up, thrusting harder and faster, as if he could no longer control his own desire.

Piper jogged her hips up to meet him, frantic for the spark that would ignite her own pleasure.

Killian slid a hand between them and toyed gently with the stiff little pearl that needed his touch.

Instantly, Piper was flying.

She cried out as the pleasure flung her out of the bed, the house, and through the clouds, then crashed her down, down, down, back into the arms of this mysterious man who was shouting out his own pleasure as he exploded inside of her.

Killian collapsed on her.

She relished the weight of him, wishing she could meld her body into his.

"Incredible," he murmured, his breath tickling her ear.

She murmured in agreement, still unable to find her own voice.

He rolled onto his side and pulled her close.

She opened her eyes and gazed up at him.

His dark eyes were sad and wondrous as he studied her

face, as if he were memorizing it, as if he were so hungry for her, he could never get his fill.

"Sleep now, my love," he whispered.

Piper wasn't sleepy. She thought she might never sleep again. But then she felt her eyes close in spite of herself.

3

PIPER

Almost two years later, Piper Lee stood in her small living room, looking around at the happy mess as baby Kieran snuggled into the crook of her neck.

She had just fed him and given him a warm bath to remove all the frosting. Now he was very sleepy.

"You're tuckered out," she murmured to him. "You ate your first cupcake, you laughed with your friends. It was a big day, birthday boy."

She stepped over a pile of crumpled wrapping paper and headed upstairs to put him to bed.

Kieran's nursery was just at the top of the steps, easy to reach from her room or the living room, with a pretty view over the trees behind the house.

She stepped in, relishing the scent of baby powder and the hint of the forest that always reminded her of his father.

Don't think about him, she cautioned herself automatically.

Honestly, it should have been easier not to think about him at this point. It had been almost two years. And he hadn't even bothered to ask her name or look her up later.

Whatever magic she thought was happening between them that night, it obviously hadn't meant anything to him.

As it turned out though, it meant everything to Piper.

"You're the best thing that ever happened to me, baby boy," she crooned.

Kieran clung to her and whimpered a little, just for show. But after the tiniest bit of consolation he settled into his crib, gripping the fuzzy bobcat he was so fond of while she rubbed his little belly.

Piper smiled down at him in the moonlight for a long time after he fell asleep.

Then she headed downstairs to clean up the mess from the party.

Allie would have stayed and cleaned up, wanted to, even.

But Piper had her pride. She wasn't going to have anyone feeling sorry for her just because she was a single parent. Caring for Kieran was a privilege. And it really was the best part of her life.

She began collecting trash and recycling, starting with the cake plates and napkins on the kitchen counter and working her way down to the ground.

When that was done, she gathered up the presents.

Kieran was only a year old, but that hadn't stopped any of his friends and relations from lavishing him with new toys.

She smiled as she picked up a fifth toy bow and arrow. It was no surprise that a couple of friends and three of the moms of her campers had bought Kieran the same gift.

As if she would ever hand any son of hers a plastic bow and arrow. Piper was planning to put a real bow in his hands as soon as he was old enough for it to be safe. She already had the perfect one picked out.

The unexpected addition of a baby to her life meant she

hadn't gone to the Olympics after all, but she loved teaching archery to the kids at the local scout camp. And as it turned out, she had a real knack for it. Maybe one day she would train an Olympic archer, or even get back into competition herself, when Kieran was older. She still practiced every day.

But her main focus for now was making a safe and happy life for her amazing son.

There was a soft sound in the baby monitor.

She walked over to it.

The video feed was fuzzy, but it was quiet again.

Still, she had a little tingle that felt oddly familiar.

Her feet carried her toward the stairs before she had fully decided to check on Kieran.

For some reason, she found herself tiptoeing in her own house, and not because she thought the baby was likely to wake up.

You just put him down, she told herself. *It's nothing.*

But her heart slammed in her chest as she approached the landing at the top of the stairs.

She was in the room before she saw it.

Someone else was in the room with her.

The large shape of a man was silhouetted against the window.

Piper lunged for the crib with all the speed she could muster.

4

———

KILLIAN

Killian held up his hand.

The woman froze, arms outstretched for the child.

This wasn't the way tonight had played out in his head.

The woman wasn't supposed to be here. She should have been asleep by now.

He wasn't supposed to see her again.

Though she could no longer move, he could see the fear and desperation in her eyes.

He glanced at the baby.

His baby.

It was a fine, healthy child. She had every right to want to protect it. He would just explain everything to her, that was all. There was no reason for her to be upset. He would explain, and then she would understand.

Then he would take the baby and leave, and he would never see her again.

And with the child in his possession, he would have someone else to love.

Perhaps the woman would stop haunting his dreams.

"Fear not, human," he said, keeping his tone smooth and modulated. He prayed all his sappy emotions would stay firmly in his chest and not escape his lips. He didn't want to sound like some lovestruck mortal.

She blinked at him, and a single tear escaped her eye and traveled down her cheek.

He closed his eyes and fought the urge to scoop it up with a finger, taste the salt of her pain.

"You may not remember me," he said lightly. "But I fathered that child. I have come to claim him so that he may take his rightful place on the throne in my world. He is a very important baby, perhaps the most important fae child in centuries."

Her eyes were wide with terror and he could sense her fighting against his magic with all her will.

Tears streamed freely down her cheeks, wetting her face and dampening the collar of her shirt.

Against his better judgement, he stepped closer and stroked her cheek.

The touch sizzled through his blood and he closed his eyes against the pleasure that surged through him. He had not tasted such sweetness since the last time they met.

What if I don't go back?

What if I stay here with the woman and child, hidden away somewhere in this realm, with none of the problems of the Autumn Court at my feet?

Pain shot through him and he opened his eyes to see that she was biting his finger.

He wrenched his hand away, cursing.

She should not have been able to fight his spell enough to do that. Her will was strong.

He grudgingly admired her fierceness, even as he sucked on his wounded finger.

He moved to the crib and looked down at his sleeping son.

The sight took his breath away.

Looking in through the window from the tree outside earlier, he'd had eyes only for the woman.

Now he was hypnotized by the beauty of his son.

The boy had dark hair, like his, and long dark lashes kissing pillowy, pale cheeks.

Killian's heart threatened to shatter.

But there was no time to moon over the child.

He slid his hands under the warm little body as gently as he could and scooped him tenderly into his arms.

The child whimpered and then buried his sweet face into Killian's neck.

Killian felt it - the shimmer of magic that assured him the child was his.

And if the babe had magic, he could serve as an heir to the Autumn Court.

Turning back to the woman, Killian noticed the letters on the wall spelling out a name.

KIERAN

HE SMILED TO HIMSELF.

For all her fear and fury, the woman had named the child with a name of his people, and one similar to his own.

"Kieran," he whispered to the downy head.

He went to the window and then turned back to the woman.

Her eyes were pure agony.

Guilt threatened to split him in half. Having held the

child, he now understood some portion of the desperate need the woman felt to protect him.

This was as it should be. She had fulfilled her duty well and her watchfulness had ensured him a healthy heir to bring back to faerie.

Any guilt he felt at not informing her of her role in the bargain needed to be pushed aside. The child was too important for Killian to succumb to such soft-hearted nonsense.

Little Kieran was going to save two kingdoms. He was more important than the woman, more important than Killian, more important than anyone or anything.

His fate was already decided.

Outside, lightning flashed, followed by a boom of thunder as rain began to streak down the window.

"After I go, you will be unfrozen," Killian told the woman gently. "Your fate will be yours once more. You have served me well. The boy is everything I could wish. Trust me when I tell you that he will have a better life than anything you could have given him, or even dreamt of. He will have a place in history. Know this, and be proud as you go on to live your own life."

She begged him without speaking, her beautiful eyes so eloquent he thought his heart would break.

With the last of his resolve, he turned on his heel and leapt out the window with the child in his arms.

5

PIPER

Piper strained against her invisible bonds as the man slipped out the window with her baby in his arms.

Stay calm. If you don't find a way to think through this, you'll never see him again...

But her heart was pounding, and she could feel the cold sweat running down her back as she prayed to every god she could think of for help.

When the spell was suddenly lifted, she nearly fell to the ground with the force of her exertions.

Piper stumbled forward and caught herself on the window ledge, scanning the ground below for broken bodies, yet knowing somehow she would not find them.

Killian and the baby were nowhere in sight.

Too late. I'm too late...

"Easy," she murmured to herself, patting her jeans pockets for her keys and trying not to think too hard about the existence of magic. That was just too much for her frantic mind to wrap itself around right now.

The keys were there, as always. She never remembered to put them in the dish by the door.

She took the stairs two at a time and flew out the front door without bothering to close it behind her.

Her old yellow VW bug was parked in the drive, sitting there calmly, as if the entire world wasn't falling apart. She clicked the button on the keychain to open the trunk and heaved out the huge canvas bag with her training equipment as the rain lashed down, sticking her hair to her cheeks.

She closed the trunk and threw the gear into the passenger's side seat before hopping in and turning the ignition.

Killian had a big head start, but he was on foot. She could beat him if her instincts were right about where he was headed.

"Don't worry, Kieran," she murmured to herself, burning rubber as she tore out of the driveway, windshield wipers barely able to keep up with the downpour. "Mama's coming."

Piper had always been diligent about driver safety. But now she just slammed her foot down on the gas and hoped that all her years of accumulated vehicular karma would pay off.

The VW's engine whined as if in complaint, but it carried her readily enough onto the main road that bisected Rosethorn Valley.

She raced deeper into the valley, and then swerved up a steep driveway, skidding slightly on the wet leaves but managing to find purchase. The little car hugged the curves of the long drive as she pushed it as fast as it would go.

"Please let me be in time, please let me be in time," she repeated to herself.

As soon as she reached her destination, she slid the car to a rough stop, and threw it into park.

She wrenched the key from the ignition, then grabbed her bag and took off, legs pumping, heart pounding, adrenaline coursing through every inch of her.

Piper was in full fight-or-flight mode.

And flight wasn't on the menu.

6

———

KILLIAN

Killian ran through the forest. It was only a mile between the woman's home and the mansion. In his other form, he would have been there already.

But the child in his arms meant he could not shift.

The warm little burden already grew heavy. But Killian could not find it in himself to resent the weight.

My son...

At last, they broke through the trees and the mansion came into view.

There was a yellow car in the driveway. He wasn't sure if it had been there before. But there were no lights on, which meant there was no one inside.

He breathed a sigh of relief and strode onto the porch. He wrapped his fingers around the brass knob of the front door, ready to release a touch of magic to charm the lock, but it was already unlocked.

"Careless," he scolded himself for forgetting to lock it on his way out. In his defense, he'd been very excited about his mission.

He opened the door and peered inside. The house was so strange on this side of the veil. So lifeless.

Killian stepped into the empty hall. The defunct grandfather clock looked over the area like a tired sentry. Moonlight bathed the black and white tiles, making it seem like he was moving across a ghostly chess board as he headed for the ballroom.

The fae realm and the human one were separated by a veil. There were places in this world and the other where the veil was thin. Rosethorn Valley, in the kingdom of Pennsylvania, was one of them. But this was not the home's original location.

This mansion had been moved, stone by stone, from Wales, all to preserve a massive mirror in the ballroom that acted more like a doorway.

Between the magic of the mirror itself, and the thinness of the veil in this little town, it was possible to step through the worlds with no magic of one's own.

As a matter of fact, during the stroke of midnight it could be done *accidentally,* even by a mortal. He'd hardly believed the tales the first time he'd heard them.

He stepped into the ballroom and drew a talisman from his pocket.

If Killian merely stepped through the mirror, he would be deposited directly into the ballroom on the other side.

But he did not wish to appear in the crowded ballroom of Midnight with a baby that he had obviously obtained in the human realm. That wouldn't do at all.

This baby's origins could not be made so clear.

To that end, Killian had obtained a talisman that would focus the magic of the mirror and allow him to appear on the roadway just outside the Autumn Court instead.

He held out the little wooden carving of the gates to the Autumn castle in one hand, still cradling the sleepy baby in the other.

The clock in the identical mansion on the other side of the veil began to strike midnight. A mist obscured his view in the huge mirror, and then it cleared to reveal a roomful of dancers at a masquerade ball.

He began to step through, knowing he would bypass the revelry and land at the gates of his own castle.

Then he heard the noise of approaching footsteps, and everything seemed to slow down.

He turned to see the mortal woman rushing at him from the shadows. She brandished something over her head, clearly intending to use it as a weapon.

He turned instinctively to protect the baby.

She brought the weapon down hard, glancing off his shoulder and smashing the small wooden gate in his hand.

"Give him back," she screamed.

But Killian couldn't reply, because suddenly, all three of them were falling, falling, through the veil and onto the other side.

He could feel it going wrong, there was never confusion like this when stepping across worlds.

But the broken little gate burned in his hand, as if trying to find its equivalent. But the magic was off.

Killian had no idea where they were going.

The mists swirled around them.

After a few more confusing seconds, he landed hard on his ass before a rusted and broken gate that he was certain he'd never seen before.

The baby whimpered on his shoulder, but they were both mercifully unharmed.

And they were home. He had no idea where, but the air was sweet and the sky was clear. Though the state of the human world impacted this one in some ways, he was thankful that the air quality was not one of them.

It worried Killian a little that the sun was up. The misfired magic must have jogged the time as well as the place of his arrival. He hoped he hadn't lost too many hours.

He glanced at the gate again. If he had to guess, he would say it looked like it belonged at one of the entrances to an old graveyard, which put them near the farthest border of the Autumn Court.

If he was right about that, this was a dangerous place, but at least he was in his own kingdom.

He got slowly to his feet, rocking slightly to encourage the child to go back to sleep.

He turned and found himself looking directly at the woman who had gotten him into this mess in the first place. In the daylight, it was easy to see what she had used to attack him in the ballroom. She was staring at him over a decidedly sharp-looking arrow, nocked in a bow that was much shorter that the ones he'd trained with in his youth.

"Put the baby down very slowly, and walk away," she growled like she meant business.

It was a false threat, but he had to give her credit for really selling it.

"Sorry," he said with a smirk. "But we both know you would never shoot me when I'm holding—"

The arrow whistled through the air and hit his thigh with a crisp *thwack.*

She shot me!

That was impossible. He looked down at the evidence protruding from his left leg that told him clearly otherwise.

Pain exploded in his thigh. He managed to hold onto the baby and shift his weight to his right ride.

"You... shot me," he said, incredulous. "In the leg."

"That was a warning," she said, nocking another arrow. "It's the only one you're going to get. Now put my baby down."

She was dead serious.

He tried to figure out how to put the baby down as carefully as possible without further injuring his leg.

She watched him warily, giving him time. But the bow didn't waver.

Killian managed to lower himself awkwardly to the ground with the baby, then set the child down beside him on the soft moss.

The boy smiled and banged his little fist on the ground.

The woman moved quick as a lightning strike, snatching up the baby and stepping away again.

He watched as she cradled the child close in her arms, crooning to him with an expression of relief and wonder as he squeaked out a joyful greeting and bopped her face with a chubby hand.

Damn it all. That was *his* baby.

"Don't move," she said icily to Killian as she placed the baby down again to sling the bow over her shoulder and across her back.

Kieran immediately began to howl from his spot in the thick grass.

"I know, buddy," she told him as she scooped him up. "You're supposed to be sleeping right now."

She turned to Killian with blazing eyes. "Where are we? Why is it the middle of the day?"

"We're in the fae realm," he told her. "I have no idea

where, because you ruined my talisman on the way through the veil."

"You kidnapped my child," she said.

"He's my child too," Killian retorted.

"How are you going to get us back?" she demanded, ignoring the very pertinent fact he had just pointed out.

"There is no way back without a considerable amount of hiking," he said. "And you've shot me in the leg."

"Aren't you supposed to be all magical or something?" she asked. "Get us out of here, *now*."

"I could leave anytime I want," he told her. "But I couldn't take the two of you with me."

"Then we'll hike," she said, firmly.

He watched as she strode fearlessly over to him.

"Take off your shirt," she said.

He arched one eyebrow.

"Take it off now," she repeated.

"My dear, I would gladly service your desires, but there's an arrow *in my leg*," he said, his voice a purr.

He really enjoyed the horrified look on her face.

"That's not what I meant," she spluttered. "Take your shirt off and give it to me so I can patch up your leg, you gigantic idiot."

He removed it slowly.

Despite the situation, there was still, almost unbelievably, tension in the air between them, as if it didn't matter that they were furious at each other, or that he was hurt. As if their bodies and hearts had no concern for what their heads and mouths might be feeling or saying.

He flung the shirt to her and she snatched it out of the air and promptly began ripping it to shreds.

"I'm making bandages," she told him. "Do you have a knife?"

Of course he had a knife. He had a powerful dagger. But he wasn't about to tell this impetuous monster of a woman about it. There was no telling what she might do with it.

"Give it to me now," she said. "I have to cut off the end of the arrow so we can get it out of you."

"I'll do it myself," he said, sliding the dagger from his boot.

She sat back on her heels and watched.

He gritted his teeth against the pain and took hold of the shaft. It was an odd thing, made of some modern, unnatural material.

Sawing through it proved an agonizing challenge but he wasn't about to show her how much it hurt. He knew he should count himself lucky that she hadn't hit bone, but somehow, he wasn't really feeling like luck was on his side right now.

At last, he managed to snap off the fletched end.

Wordlessly, she helped him roll onto his side.

"Brace yourself," she said, in the gentlest voice she had used on him yet.

He had just enough time to wonder if she would hurt him purposefully.

She grasped the arrowhead on the back of his thigh with her hand wrapped in his shirt and yanked it, firm and true.

The thing slid out of him and he nearly groaned with the mingled pain and relief.

Then there was a thunder of muted agony as she put pressure on both sides of the wound.

"Dammit, woman," he croaked.

"Hold still," she advised him. "I don't have anything to disinfect with. We don't want anything extra getting in."

Gods, but she had a powerful grip.

Kieran, meanwhile, had found a bright green leaf. He was waving it around and laughing.

Killian distracted himself slightly with his son's mirth.

At last, the woman seemed to be satisfied. She began binding his leg tightly with the rags that seemed to be the only remnants of his shirt.

When she was finished, she sat back to admire her handiwork.

He had to admit it, wasn't badly done.

She grabbed the dagger from beside his hand and shoved it in her belt loop.

"Okay, let's get you up," she told him.

"Not without my dagger," he said, hand out.

"I don't think so," she said. "You're as weak as a lamb and may need my support. I can't come close if you're armed with a dagger and I only have a bow."

He could hardly argue with that cold-minded logic.

He allowed her to help him up, peevishly not putting forth as much effort as he could have just to be difficult. She struggled, but it didn't bring him nearly as much joy as he hoped it would.

After he was on his feet, she scooped up the baby who laughed and waved the leaf at her.

"That's awesome, Kieran," she said.

Killian tested out his injured leg. It hurt to put weight on it, but it would hold him.

The woman rummaged around in the trees and came back to him carrying a solid ash stick.

"This should help," she said, handing it over.

"I suppose you are waiting for my thanks, woman, after you injured me in the first place," he sniffed.

"My name is not *woman*," she said. "It's Piper. Now get me home."

Piper...

He hadn't wanted to know her name.

And now he hated himself. He hated himself for standing here, bleeding, in a dangerous place, while she glared at him with all the hate of hellfire, knowing he wanted her more than he had the night he'd first seen her through the veil and had to have her.

Piper, you're mine...

7

______

PIPER

Piper gazed into the beautiful, serene eyes of her baby's father and wished that she could smash him over the head with something, preferably something heavy.

Unfortunately, Killian was her only way out of this place. She would have to put her head-smashing fantasy on hold until he got her and baby Kieran home.

"Come on," she said in a businesslike way as she headed for the gate, hoping maybe they could glean some information from it.

"Don't go that way," he warned her. "It's dangerous."

"You just don't want me to figure out where I am," she said lightly, continuing onward. "Don't try to play me for a fool. Kieran and I will find our way out of here, even without you, if we have to."

"Kieran is staying in Faerie," Killian roared.

"Over my dead body," Piper retorted.

"If necessary, yes," Killian said.

His voice was like ice, but something about the way he

looked away when he said it made her think he might actually feel a little bad about it.

Good. He should feel bad. He tried to steal my baby.

She reached the gate and studied it. There were no words, but a few symbols she didn't recognize adorned the posts.

She crouched to get a better look at them.

Kieran leaned forward in her arms to grasp at the peeling paint.

"No, baby," she told him, grabbing the little hand.

"It's a graveyard," Killian said from right behind her.

"That must mean we're close to civilization," she said, straightening up.

"Quite the opposite," he told her. "We don't keep our dead close like you do. They don't always sleep as lightly. Graveyards here are on the borders."

Piper didn't want to think about exactly what that might mean.

"The borders of what?" she asked.

"Kingdoms," he told her simply. "This must be the border between the Summer and Autumn Courts. See how dry the grass is over there? And there's a warm breeze, with just the slightest edge to it."

"Which court do you belong to?" she asked.

"Autumn," he told her after a brief pause.

"So you know how to get me home from there?" she asked, purposefully not mentioning Kieran. The man was crazy if he thought there was any way she was leaving without her baby, but there was no need to force the issue right now.

Killian studied her for a moment and then nodded.

"Let's go then," she said, heading into the graveyard.

"Piper, no," he called to her.

"Help me or watch me," she offered over her shoulder.

"You don't understand," he yelled. "Get back here, right now."

Did he still think he was the boss of her? Piper wasn't about to start taking orders from him, even if she didn't really have any idea where she was going. It was time for her to take the lead, and she was reasonably sure that if she started off, he would follow her.

And if the graveyard was on the border then going through it ought to get her closer to their destination. She was heading in the opposite direction of the dry grass that signified the Summer Court. Although the temperature did seem to dip substantially as soon as the trees closed in overhead.

She picked up her pace to a light jog, holding Kieran close. The soil was soft beneath her feet and the shaded cemetery was filled with a silence that was almost palpable.

She ran past a marble angel. The pedestal it sat on was covered in vines with tiny purple flowers. The angel's arms extended toward heaven, but its chin was tilted downward, as if it were looking for something. Peculiar rusty stains on its brow gave it an angry expression.

Piper shivered. There was something super creepy about it, even for a cemetery.

Kieran clung to her quietly, as if he too sensed there was something off about this place.

It hit Piper suddenly that maybe the silence was the real issue. Killian should be following her by now.

She turned back to find nothing but empty graveyard as far as she could see. Even the lone bird's nest in the nearby tree looked long-vacated.

"Coward," she muttered to herself - Killian, that was, not

the birds. She couldn't blame them for getting out of this unsettling place.

At least she had managed to escape with Kieran. That was lucky. And maybe she didn't really need Killian as much as he seemed to think. Maybe she could find some other faerie to help her get back to her own realm.

Never bargain with a faerie.

That was like the first rule in all of the children's storybooks. But clearly Piper was well past that.

I had a baby with a fae man.

Did that really make Kieran half-fae? She wondered vaguely if her baby had the magic to get them home again.

Then she laughed at herself inwardly.

Her sweet baby boy was one hundred percent human. Of course he was. If he had any kind of magic, she would know it by now.

You can't hide that kind of thing from your mom.

She had been jogging a long time now, but if Killian wasn't following her, she figured she could slow down a bit. The baby was getting heavy and it wasn't like she had brought a carrier with her.

She slowed to a brisk walk and spotted another statue not too far in front of her - another creepy angel. Great. This place certainly had a motif going.

As she drew closer, she noticed the rust stains on its brow and the purple-flowered vines climbing the pedestal.

It wasn't another creepy angel.

This was the *same* one.

"That's impossible," she murmured to herself. She had been running in a straight line, definitely not a circle. She wasn't that confused.

She looked back to find an identical view to what she'd seen before, right down to the abandoned bird's nest.

This was definitely the same statue. And the sun was sinking in the sky, which showed she'd been walking for a while.

Suddenly, her legs were trembling from a combination of nerves and exhaustion, and she felt herself on the verge of tears.

She lowered herself to the edge of the pedestal.

Sit for a minute, catch your breath, don't panic.

She sat and Kieran mercifully cuddled closer, letting her rest. The vines made such a soft cushiony seat.

I'll just close my eyes for a minute...

Piper awoke to the sound of someone roaring and cursing.

She tried to jerk upright, but found she couldn't move at all.

She had no idea how long she'd been out, but the vines had begun to grow all around her, lashing her to the marble angel statue. She peered out through the tangle of leaves, the perfume of the delicate purple blooms making her feel even sleepier than before.

Over her, Killian was tearing at the vines with all his strength, trying to free her.

"Dagger, in my boot," she murmured groggily.

She felt him fighting through the vines, digging around near her foot.

Kieran was snoring softly in the crook of her neck, clearly unconcerned about the whole business.

At last, something slid out of her boot.

Then Killian was slashing the vines, grabbing her bodily, wrenching her with all his might until she felt herself finally pull free.

She stumbled a few yards away from the statue.

The remaining fragments of vine on her sizzled and

turned to ash, their dust shimmering slightly as it fell to the ground.

"What *was* that?" she asked.

"Dream root," Killian said gruffly. "I told you this place was dangerous."

Kieran chuckled and put his arms out to him.

He never did that to anyone. He was usually very wary, especially of strangers.

Killian's fierce expression melted into a lovesick smile.

"I thought you were trying to trick me," Piper said, clutching the baby closer.

"That tracks," Killian said, glancing up from the baby to make eye contact with her. "I've been known to be dangerous myself."

A frisson of awareness shot through her and she looked away from him.

"Come on, love," he said quietly. "Let's get back to the Autumn Court. We have a long way to go."

"I will not go with you if you are trying to make me go home without Kieran," she said softly. "I would rather die right here."

8

KILLIAN

Killian sighed and ran a hand through his hair.

As a child, he had learned courtly manners as well as hunting and trigonometry. He knew agrarian practices for his region and even how to command a ship at war. The education of a fae prince was nothing if not rigorous.

But none of his tutors had ever taught him what to do in this situation.

"I'll explain while we walk," he told her at last, figuring the truth was his last resort.

She was too fearless to accept anything less, and she wasn't ready to leave without the child. Maybe if he could make her see how important Kieran was to be to this world, she might begin to understand.

"There are four courts of the seasons," he began. This part was easy, every school child knew it. "My kingdom, the Court of Autumn, is the domain of the harvest, of change, of golden light before the winter."

He glanced over and she nodded her understanding. She wasn't a dullard. That was good.

"The Court of Summer is a riotous kingdom," he went on. "It is the court of color, of excess, of unfettered pleasure."

They reached a small ravine and he offered her his arm.

She shook her head and jumped over, baby and all. She was surprisingly strong and agile for a human.

Killian used his stick to launch himself over. She wasn't the only one who was athletic, even if his leg slowed him down a bit. That was hardly his fault. He hadn't shot himself.

"Your realm impacts ours," he went on. "Your careless poisoning of your environment blurs the line between fall and winter in your world. And then it happens here as well. The Winter King and the Autumn King are feuding."

"What does that have to do with Kieran?" she asked.

"I am a Prince of Autumn," he replied. "It is my sole duty to take a Winter Princess as my betrothed and sire an heir on her."

"If you do that, what do you need with my son?" Piper demanded.

My son... our son.

He pressed his lips together. This part was surprisingly hard to tell her, even though he knew how much she hated him.

"I am already betrothed," he said quietly.

"Wait, you're *engaged?*" she asked incredulously. "Were you... never mind."

"It was arranged by our parents before we ever met," he explained. "There is a prophecy that tells of the mounting animosity among our courts. It is said that a daughter of Winter will bring peace to both kingdoms. It is her destiny."

Piper didn't look convinced. Mortals never were much for prophecies.

"But yes," he told her. "Princess Wynter will one day be

my wife. You would probably get along with her well. She hates me almost as much as you do."

Piper only scowled at him.

"At any rate," he continued. "The fae are not always known to be fertile. And as I said, my betrothed despises me, which further complicates matters. Our marriage has not been, and will not be, consummated. As my only recourse, I came to your world to father a child which will serve as our heir. Kieran will be adored by everyone in both kingdoms. He will live a life of luxury you cannot imagine. And he will save our kingdoms from war."

He glanced over.

Her brow was furrowed, her lips brushing Kieran's dark curls unconsciously.

She wasn't saying no.

"What if I said I would allow this," she said at last. "But only if I can come with him?"

He opened his mouth to roar at her, and then closed it again.

She was closer to a yes now, he had to be careful. It would solve a lot of his problems if he could convince her to just go along with his plan.

"Fae court is dangerous," he said. "For anyone, but more so for a human."

"Then how can you keep Kieran safe?" she asked, clutching him even closer.

"First of all, he's an heir to both Autumn and Winter," he said. "He will have power of his own. And also, he's not human."

"Of course he's human," Piper retorted looking down at the child in her arms.

"Not fully," Killian said.

"That's ridiculous," she replied, but she sounded less certain.

"I could sense the magic on him the moment I saw him," Killian told her gently. "If I hadn't, I would have left him sleeping in his crib. He'll show you when he's ready."

"I'm coming with him," she repeated.

"You can't come with him," he told her. "Having his mortal mother at his side would defeat the entire purpose of my mission. And you would be despised for who you were."

She looked completely lost and exhausted.

In spite of everything, he hated to see anything like defeat in her eyes.

"I know he gets heavy," he said. "Would you permit me to carry him for a little while?"

But she only wrapped her arms tighter around the baby and turned her face away from him.

Killian looked away in shame, and spotted something moving in the trees.

"Stop," he whispered, throwing an arm in front of her to prevent her movement, in case she was too headstrong to listen this time.

She followed his sightline and gasped slightly when she saw what he was looking at.

Ahead of them, at the edge of the path they were on, a massive boar observed them from the trees, half shrouded in shadow.

"I need my bow," she whispered.

The creature was still too far away to be a threat. But it was blocking the path they needed to travel, and that would be a problem.

She was right, the bow was the best bet. Maybe if she fired a few shots in its direction, she could frighten it away.

Or maybe she would enrage it, and it would charge.

If that happened, they were in trouble. He'd seen men come back seriously wounded, or even killed, from much smaller boars. One of his groundskeepers still walked with a limp from tangling with one half this size.

Killian could probably dispatch it with his dagger, but he was already wounded. He would have to let it get far too close for what he was capable of in this state.

And between his injured leg and the baby, there was no way they could outrun it. Maybe it would just move away and let them pass.

The beast stepped out of the shadows and lifted its horrible snout into the air, tusks gleaming madly in the last of the twilight sun. It glared at them, and Killian could sense the challenge in its eyes. They must have wandered right into its territory.

So much for just letting them pass.

"You're going to have to trust me," Killian said, his voice barely a whisper. "Hand me the baby, or hand me the bow."

She looked down at Kieran and then over at Killian.

"If you move even one inch with him, I'll shoot you again," she told him.

"I believe you," he said.

She held out Kieran to him, her arms trembling. Killian wondered if she was making the right choice. Her arms must be exhausted from carrying the baby. Killian had always excelled in his archery lessons. Even on a bad leg, he was sure he could land a shot on the beast before it reached them.

But there was no time to argue now. He reached out and took the baby in his arms. Kieran laughed and smacked Killian on the nose. He pulled his son in close, already feeling almost drunk on his enchanting smell.

When he looked back, Piper already had an arrow

nocked and ready. Her arm trembled slightly with the effort of drawing the bow.

This was a mistake.

"Have you ever shot a boar before?" he asked.

She shook her head slightly.

"They're surprisingly fast," he warned her. "You won't get a second shot."

She gasped.

The boar was already charging, snorting, mouth frothing with the effort behind the flash of hooves.

Piper's eyes narrowed and she pressed her lips together as her gaze turned to ice.

She loosed a shot. But it was too early, the boar was still too far away. Her only shot would be wasted.

Killian watched the arrow cut through the air and find its mark right between the wretched monster's eyes. But he didn't have time to be impressed, because the beast still charged, too stubborn to realize it was already dead.

Piper's hands were a blur. Before he could register what she was doing, she had drawn and fired again.

This time, she struck the creature in one of its front legs, breaking its gait and causing it to stumble.

Its momentum carried it forward the last few paces and it collapsed, twitching, at their feet.

Killian let out a breath he hadn't realized he'd been holding, and suddenly felt much better about her choice to hand him the baby instead of the bow.

9

—————

PIPER

An hour later, Piper sat on the soft ground, nursing Kieran while Killian fussed with the hunk of boar meat roasting over the fire.

A week ago, she wouldn't have believed she would want to eat an animal that had just attacked her. But right now, she was hungry enough to eat almost anything. And this particular, slow-roasting beast smelled delightful.

"I know your kind doesn't typically like this much intimacy with its main course," Killian said, as if reading her mind.

"I'm getting dinner and revenge at the same time," Piper joked. "What could be better?"

"Literally anything cooked by someone else, with the proper tools and spices," Killian said gruffly. "I'm doing my best, but my cook at court would make this indescribably delicious."

"Well, I'm indescribably hungry," she told him. "So I'm sure it will be delicious to me."

It was hard to be mad at a man who was cooking for her.

And harder still to be mad while she was feeding the baby, which always made her feel cozy and peaceful.

Kieran fell off her breast and she slid her shirt down and got him up on her shoulder where he let out a terrific burp.

"That feels better," Piper praised him.

"What's wrong with him?" Killian asked, sounding a little horrified.

"That was just a burp," she said.

"Wasn't it... kind of loud, with him being so small?" he asked.

"It was one of his quieter burps," she said, laughing. "After you spend a little more time with us, you'll see."

"Hm," Killian said, rubbing his chin.

"What does that mean?" Piper asked.

"It means I think I might have found a way around our disagreement," he said.

"What disagreement is that?" she asked.

"You know," he said. "What to do about the baby."

"There is no disagreement," she said. "This is my son. I've raised him, and I'm not giving him up. If you mean you've found a solution that prevents you from trying to kidnap him and getting yourself shot again, I'm all ears."

Killian sighed.

But Piper didn't feel a bit sorry for him. He had a lot of nerve, acting exasperated when he was the one trying to take her child.

"Listen, woman—" he began.

"Piper," she corrected him.

"Listen, Piper," he said. "I think I know what we can do. You can come home with me to the Autumn Court and you can stay with the child. But not as his mother - as his wet nurse."

She opened her mouth to argue, but then shut it again. That actually wasn't the worst idea.

"That way," Killian added, "you could still spend most of your time by his side."

"What happens when he stops nursing?" she asked.

"We'll deal with it when it happens," he said. "But it will be a while. Fae children nurse until their third birthday."

"So I spend the next two years nursing him and taking care of him when you and your wife don't want him?" Piper asked.

"My betrothed, not my wife," he said. "And yes, exactly. She won't want him often. She's not fond of children. Or most adults, frankly. Your real job will be to endear yourself to the court so that when the time comes, you'll be kept on as his nanny."

"And how do I do that?" she asked.

"Damned if I know," he admitted, rubbing the back of his neck. "The Autumn Court can be rough. You have to understand that. We deal in loss and transition."

That didn't sound good.

"But we're also... sentimental, I guess you'd call it," he said. "Your devotion to the boy will appeal to many."

Great.

"Will you do it?" he asked. "Will you come with us?"

Something in his expression reminded her of her son for an instant, and she nearly gasped.

"Please, Piper," he said, crouching down before her and wincing at the pain in his leg. "It's the only way. I've got two kingdoms on the brink of war. Please, help me."

She had been ready to turn her back on him forever. But that seemed much easier when he was trying to abduct her baby than it was now, when he was genuinely asking for help for the good of his people.

"Will you promise to protect me?" she asked.

"Are you offering me a bargain?" he asked, his bright eyes suddenly twinkling. "Didn't your mother ever warn you not to bargain with the fae?"

"No," Piper said. "She never did. And I don't even know why I just asked for your promise, your promises clearly mean nothing."

She clamped her mouth shut, hating herself for still resenting his disappearance almost two years ago.

"What's that supposed to mean?" he demanded.

"Nothing," she said, turning away.

"I know you keep going on and on about me stealing your son," he said. "But you seem to conveniently forget that he's my son, too."

"That's *not* what I meant," she said. "And he might be biologically yours, but you haven't been there. And that makes him mine."

He studied her for a long moment.

"I see," he said at last.

There was a strange moment of awkwardness between them.

"I need to find a place for him to rest," Piper said, indicating the baby, who was asleep on her shoulder.

Killian nodded.

A moment later, she felt a strange sort of hush in the air.

She turned to find a blanket of golden leaves swirling as if caught in a tiny tornado. Except that there was no breeze at all.

Killian watched the leaves, enjoying her surprise.

His right index finger swirled and then made a smoothing motion.

The leaves rustled gently into place, so many layers they formed a bed.

Piper didn't want to show she was impressed, she really didn't. But it was too amazing not to investigate.

"Good enough in a pinch?" Killian asked.

She nodded, and gently lowered Kieran down to his leafy bower.

The little one whimpered once with a furrowed brow. But when Piper laid her hand on his belly, his forehead smoothed and he drifted off, looking contented.

"Thank you," she said quietly to Killian.

He winced a little at that. She wasn't sure why.

"He's a good lad," he said, gazing down at her son.

Their son.

She felt a pang in her chest.

It wasn't that Kieran wasn't enough. He was. But there had already been so many amazing moments when she wished she had someone to share her pride and wonder at this incredible boy.

"So, I broke a promise to you?" Killian asked, lowering himself to sit beside her.

"Not really," she said, feeling embarrassed.

"You mean the night we were together," he said gruffly.

They sat quietly for a long time, watching the fire crackle and dance.

"You're right," he said at last. "It did feel like a promise. It was a promise, or at least it would have been, if things were different."

"Look, I just don't do things like that," she said. "That's all. You don't have to pretend it was a big deal for you, too."

"You don't do things like what?" he asked.

"You know," she said. "I don't sleep with guys I just met. Usually. But I know one-night stands are no big deal for a lot of people. You're not supposed to make a big thing out of it."

His eyes flashed and she couldn't tell if it was with fury or recognition.

"If it were up to me," he told her, his voice low, "I would have claimed you permanently that night."

10

———

KILLIAN

The woman, Piper, blinked up at him, unbelieving.

Instinct took over and Killian did the only thing he knew he shouldn't.

He cupped her cheek with one hand and bent to kiss her.

After all he'd seen her do today, he knew he'd be lucky if she only cuffed him and didn't sink a blade into him for such a transgression.

But instead, she kissed him back with a muted fury.

He groaned and fed on her mouth, trying to absorb everything about her - her soft mouth, her coconut scent, the tickle of her long hair against his hand.

She made a tiny whimpering sound and he pulled back regretfully.

But when he looked into her eyes, he only saw his own need reflected back.

"I want you so much," he heard himself tell her. "I've missed you every hour."

"Why did you leave?" she whispered, breaking his heart. "You didn't even say good-bye."

"I was afraid," he admitted. "I was afraid I wouldn't have the strength. I was afraid of what was between us. And I still am."

"What's between us?" she murmured, her eyes hazy with something like lust.

"Destiny," he whispered. "It's a binding of souls, the pull that mates a couple for life. You must feel it, too."

Her eyes widened, but she didn't try to deny it.

"This is why you *slept* with me after we first met," he told her, trying to use her language, though it paled in comparison to how he would have described what they had done. "Even if it was against your nature. This is why you kept the boy, in spite of the circumstances of his conception."

"Of course I kept him," Piper said, looking like she was about to be angry again.

"That's not what I meant," he said quickly. "I mean you *never* considered giving him up, even before you saw him."

She nodded and he knew she understood. It would be common for a young single woman to consider her options. But Piper never had. She had instinctively clung to their bond, even when she hadn't been planning to start a family. Even though it must have derailed many of her life plans.

"I wanted to check in on you," he told her. "But I couldn't, not when I felt this way about you. My mission had been to father a child to be a fae heir, not to bind my soul to a mortal."

"So this was on purpose?" she asked.

He looked down at his hands, preparing himself for her anger.

"I hope you will understand that I am sacrificing my own life and happiness for the same cause," he told her quietly. "Our sacrifices will save many thousands of lives. But to solidify a treaty, Wynter and I need an heir."

Her eyes narrowed at the mention of his betrothed. Was that... jealousy he saw there?

"So why didn't you just make one with her?" Piper asked.

"You don't understand," he told her, shaking his head. "There are lots of reasons. First of all, the fae are not as fertile as humans. It could take decades to conceive, or it might never happen. Secondly, Wynter will never take me into her bed."

"Didn't you say you were betrothed?" Piper asked.

"She hates me," he replied. "I wasn't kidding about that. She has a bevy of pretty serving boys who take care of her needs. My job is to stay out of her way and make peace between our kingdoms. Our heir will be accepted as true, so long as we make any effort to present him as such. It's actually not all that uncommon among arranged royal marriages."

Killian glanced over instinctively at Kieran asleep on the golden leaves. His heart throbbed at the beauty of the babe, and the perfect balance he struck between his father's dark hair and his mother's soft cheeks.

"He's incredible, isn't he?" Piper said.

"He is incredible," Killian agreed. "I'm sorry I haven't been there. I will make it up to him. And I will try to find a way to make it up to you."

She turned back to him, a curious expression in her eyes.

"So you're not looking to be his dad in the same way you're expecting to be a husband?" she asked.

He blinked at her in shock. "Of course not," he breathed.

"I was afraid you wanted him only as an heir," she said.

So she thought that he would take him merely so he could exist in the Autumn Court, a spoiled little prince raised by nannies, separate from him, a solution to a prob-lem. That could not be further from the truth.

But it made sense. He certainly hadn't given her any reason to think otherwise.

"I will love him," Killian said. "I love him already."

She smiled at him then, and it was the most beautiful thing he had ever seen.

"Piper," he breathed, reaching out to stroke her cheek.

She leaned into his touch.

"I don't know what's happening to me," she said softly. "I want to hate you, I want to go home and forget all this."

But her lips were brushing his palm and he was biting back a sob of relief that she wanted him.

"We can never truly go back," he told her. "Our fates are one. You and the boy will be by my side, under my protection. I will bring you happiness."

She smiled and he wondered if she heard it too, the echo of the first words he had ever said to her.

I'm going to show you pleasure you cannot imagine...

In his ignorance, he hadn't understood the complexity of what those words truly meant. There was physical pleasure, yes, wild enough he was afraid he would lose his senses to it.

But there was also the pleasure of watching their sleeping child. And the pleasure of the pride he felt when his bold mate slew a wild boar with a fierceness that matched any warrior he'd ever met. There was the pleasure of sharing her company before the fire.

She tilted her chin up, and closed her eyes to be kissed.

A surge of love threatened to blast his heart out of his ribcage. He kissed her wildly, thoroughly, until both of them were trembling with need.

"Piper," he murmured again, pulling her down so that they both lay on the soft ground, stars dotting the sky above.

She kissed him again, warm and willing, sending his senses reeling.

11

PIPER

Piper let herself go.

It was like a dream, the cool fall air, the twinkling stars, the warm hands of her lover, slowly removing her clothing until she was bare to him under the midnight sky.

"Beautiful," he murmured.

Her body was different from last time, fuller in the breasts and belly. There were lines at her navel that radiated out from the place where her body had stretched to bring about a miracle - like a child's emphasis marks around a drawing of a super hero.

But she felt no embarrassment. Piper was proud of every curve and line. She had come about them in the best way, they were a mark of honor.

Besides, she could read Killian's approval in his hungry eyes.

He bent to nuzzle her breasts, flicking his tongue over her dark nipples.

She closed her eyes and tried not to moan.

Then he was kissing his way down her belly, pressing his lips reverently against her navel as he made his way down.

She was ready, too ready. It was as if her body had been simmering for him all this time, ready to boil over at the slightest touch.

He nudged her thighs apart impatiently.

She opened her eyes to see his dark head between her legs and then she let her head fall back against the mossy ground once more.

Killian pressed a kiss against her tender sex.

She moaned and felt her hips lift to meet his mouth.

He licked her slowly, firmly, as if trying to prolong her pleasure.

Piper whimpered and shivered, losing herself to sensation.

Killian continued his slow, teasing exploration, bringing her closer and closer to satisfaction, but never allowing it.

Piper felt her whole body tensing, her need balancing her on the precipice.

"Please," she whispered at last.

He growled against her and slid a thick finger slowly inside her.

She felt herself throb helplessly on him as he licked around his finger, at first slowly and then faster.

Behind Piper's eyelids, stars exploded, and worlds formed and reformed.

Killian began to move his hand slowly, while he flicked her stiff little bud firmly with his tongue.

Piper cried out and the world shattered around her with the force of her ecstasy.

Killian continue to feed on her, extending the shivering pleasure until she could take no more.

"Killian," she whispered, putting her arms out to him.

He crawled slowly up to her, his mouth glistening.

She reached for the cord that fastened his breeches. His need was bulging against the leather, making her hungry inside all over again.

But he stayed her hand and kissed her forehead, before lying beside her and pulling her close.

"Don't you want...?" she whispered plaintively.

"I want you more than you can know," he murmured. "But we cannot give that child a sibling. At least, not until it's safe."

Piper hadn't thought about that. She had not been thinking about anything, except the frantic need to feel him inside her.

"Rest now, love," he murmured to her, stroking her shoulder blades. "This time, I will be here when you wake."

12

WYNTER

Wynter pulled the hateful fur cloak around herself, disguising her slender form under the bulky garment as she stole the last few steps through the woods to her clandestine meeting.

It was bad enough that she had to leave the palace and appear at this horrible little cottage. But it was truly hell not to flaunt the wildly expensive silken gown she wore underneath.

She had heard that pregnancy was ghoulish, and she believed it. Even hiding in her chambers for months *pretending* to be pregnant was hideously dreadful.

"Here, my queen," Berit whispered servilely, indicating the ugly cottage with a flourish, as if she'd been too blind to see it.

It was so hard to find good manservants.

His brother, Baird, scowled as if he wished he'd thought of introducing her to something that was right in front of her nose. Then he gestured as well, inclining his head so that his blond hair shone white in the moonlight.

"I'm not a queen yet," she sniffed.

"But soon you will be," Baird whispered seductively.

These two jokers were lucky they were handsome, even if they were jealous of each other over her attentions. Toying with her attendants was one of her only pastimes, now that she was in her pretend confinement.

She rolled her eyes and banged on the door to the cottage, half-expecting the whole dilapidated building to collapse under her hand.

"Come in," a rough voice barked.

She stepped back, disgusted, while Berit and Baird stumbled over themselves to open the door for her.

These mercenaries were expecting a princess of the Winter Court, betrothed to a prince of the Autumn Court. One would think they could bother themselves to get up to let her in.

Though perhaps their studied flaunting of protocol was meant to show her they were truly mercenaries - respecting only the sovereignty of coin.

Well, lucky for them, she had that in spades.

Baird managed to yank the doorknob from his brother's hand and the door swung open to reveal the small and filthy interior. It looked like a hunting lodge after a party. Empty bottles littered the floor.

There was no baby here, she could see that at once. Every inch of the horrible little place was on full display.

And with that realization, her last hope, that they had taken their quarry and simply not brought it to her yet, was dashed.

A mountain of a man with an eyepatch sat at one end of the table. An even larger man in a grimy suit jacket and dungarees sat at the other.

She imagined they must have names, but she certainly wasn't about to learn them.

"Yer Majesty," Suit Jacket said, slowly rising, as if to show her he didn't have to extend this courtesy.

"Please," said Eyepatch. "Have a seat."

She surveyed the bench he was pointing at.

"I'll stand," she decided.

"Suit yourself," he shrugged. "What's your business?"

What was her business? She had paid them good coin already, through her attendants, to do the job.

And they hadn't done it yet.

"I was told you were discrete men who would take a bounty without a fuss," she said crisply.

"*Discrete men*," Suit Jacket snorted.

Eyepatch joined him in a laugh. "Aye, lass, we're that alright."

"I hired you to collect the babe at the gates," she said through a clenched jaw. "Where is it?"

"There was no babe," Eyepatch said sullenly.

"He came through without the child?" she asked.

That didn't track. Her idiotic betrothed had been beside himself with excitement about collecting the stupid thing.

"Nothing came through," Suit Jacket said.

"So I hired the most expensive goons in the kingdom, and you came up empty-handed?" she asked.

"You hired the most expensive goons in *four* kingdoms," Eyepatch said, picking something out from between two of his yellow teeth. "But we're not magicians. We can't collect something that isn't there."

"I'm not impressed," she said coldly. "What are you doing here? Why aren't you waiting at the gates."

"You want us to wait in ambush again, the fee is the same as before," Eyepatch said.

She nearly choked with surprise.

"That's our daily rate, Majesty," Suit Jacket pointed out helpfully. "We're busy men. Our time is very valuable."

She wanted nothing more than to bash their stupid heads together.

"It's too late to wait by the gates," she said, pacing the horrible cottage. "Something must have gone wrong. His meddling brother is already leading a secret search party to find him. I assumed you had simply taken him out in the struggle."

The two dunces just stared at her.

"You're going to have to search for him, too," she said. "Find them first. Bring the baby to me. If Killian doesn't make it back, that's fine."

"They have the edge," Eyepatch pointed out. "They began searching first."

"Are you saying you need my help?" she asked.

His eyes widened.

She peeled the velvet glove from her right hand and retrieved the talisman from a hidden pocket.

It was an intricate depiction of a small dog, formed from an ice-blue diamond, surrounded by a delicate circle of pure silver that had been covered in ancient runes. A fine silver chain dangled from the top.

The magic it contained rushed through her blood, icy and pure even in this filthy abode.

The men around her gasped as pale blue light sizzled in her palm and shot out to the floor in front of her, forming a small orb, then growing larger.

First the barrel-like torso formed, an oval and circle expanding down into four thick muscular legs. Then the head popped out, long slender snout, ears pinned back from a sinister, sneering face.

The hellhound landed with lightning arcing from its

paws along the disgusting floor of the hovel as it began to take on weight and reality. Blue fire turned to black fur and thick muscles.

A moment later it was a very real and snarling hound, snapping at Tweedle Dee and Tweedle Dum, who nearly knocked over the table trying to get out of its way.

The hellhound turned back to Wynter with pure hate in its eyes. It was clearly angry at being summoned, and would like nothing better than to rip out the throat of the person responsible. Its sinewy muscles bunched as it prepared to pounce.

But Wynter calmly held the talisman before her, and the beast lowered its head in supplication, bringing a cruel smile to Wynter's face.

As long as the rune-covered silver encased the diamond carving of the hound, whoever possessed the talisman would be the creature's unquestionable master.

She slipped the long silver chain over her neck, then reached a gloved hand into her pocket and withdrew a heavy, iron lead.

She flicked it outward, and it magically fastened itself around the beast's neck, causing it to cry out in pain. Fae creatures, even brutes like this one, abhorred the touch of cold iron. It was a crude solution, but it would bring the beast to heel for the unprotected men.

She tossed her end of the lead to Eyepatch, who had the presence of mind to pull his own hand inside his sleeve before grabbing it.

"Will that be enough help for you?" she asked coldly.

"D-does it track?" Eyepatch asked, cowed at last.

She bent to offer the beast a whiff of the handkerchief Killian had given her at their first meeting.

She had coughed and he'd made a big deal out of the

polite gesture, proving what she had already known, that he was a boring, nice guy.

Wynter preferred war.

Her intended marriage to Killian was supposed to broker some sort of peace between the two kingdoms, there was a whole prophecy about it. And producing an heir would seal the deal. But she had other plans.

All she needed to topple the tenuous peace was to ensure the subjects of the Winter Court thought that soldiers from the Autumn Court had kidnapped Wynter and Killian's heir. After that, war would be inevitable.

It was too bad these two oafs were the best men she could find for the job. The thugs were already trembling in their boots, as the creature stared them down.

"Get. The. Child," she ordered.

"Majesty, it will be done," Suit Jacket said.

"I'm not holding my breath," she sniffed. "And don't let the other search party see you."

"Ahem," Eyepatch coughed. "There's the matter of our fee."

The utter nerve. She wanted nothing more than to silence him with the sweet agony of a slow death.

Remember why you are here. The future dominance of Winter Court depends on it.

The words echoed in her head. It felt like a thousand years since her father had sent her here to rot among the sappy fools of the Autumn Court.

"Berit," she said, waving her hand. "Baird, with me."

Berit scurried forward to settle her accounts with the two thugs.

Baird, sensing his advantage, opened the cottage door with a flourish, letting in a welcome gust of fresh, cool air.

Soon, she told herself, as they set back toward the castle.

Soon this whole disgusting mess will be over, and the sweet sounds of war will fill the air again.

The Winter Court was growing too warm from mortal carelessness.

But if Winter took control of Autumn's lands, they could cool them further, providing a buffer against the encroaching heat.

Fall was overrated anyway. They would be doing the fae realm a favor.

13

KILLIAN

Killian awoke bathed in happiness.

Once Piper had fallen asleep, he had collected the babe and placed him gently between them. Then he had closed his eyes and allowed himself to slip into his animal form.

Instantly, the pain from the arrow wound retreated, and the pain of desiring his mate faded somewhat as well.

His senses of smell and hearing heightened in exchange, allowing him to rest in the knowledge that he could sense a predator coming for miles in any direction.

He would have liked to have loped through the trees and found a small rabbit.

But he had a youngling to mind.

He stretched gloriously instead, and curled his body around the child, who slept in the curve of his mother's back.

Satisfied that the little one was safe and warm, he had promptly fallen into a deep sleep.

Now that he was awake, he stretched again, luxuriating

in the feel of the smooth muscles extending under his glossy fur.

"*Ba*," Kieran cried beside him.

He opened his eyes to find his son observing him with delight.

Little hands grabbed onto his fur, but it didn't hurt even when Kieran used that leverage to pull himself all the way up to sitting.

"*Ca, ca, ca*," Kieran said importantly, banging on his father's haunches.

It dawned on him that the child was saying *cat*.

And he was correct. His father was in the form of a lynx right now. Smart boy.

Killian gave the babe a gentle head butt, which sent the boy off into trills of laughter.

Killian was so taken with the child's amusement that he did not notice Piper stirring until it was too late.

Suddenly she was snatching up the baby and backing toward her bow.

Kieran wailed at the loss of his new playmate as Killian flung himself into the change, rising so quickly into his human form that it almost made him dizzy.

"K-Killian?" Piper stammered.

"Yes," he said as calmly as he could. "Sleeping in my animal form allowed my wound to heal. And it's easier to protect the baby and keep him warm as a lynx. I forgot that it might be startling. I should have warned you."

"So it *was* you," she said to herself, still clutching Kieran, who waved his little arms at Killian like he was directing traffic.

"What do you mean?" Killian asked.

"At the party," she said. "I thought I saw a big cat in the mirror. That's why I went into the hall."

"Yes, it was me," he admitted with a smile. "My brother has been calling me the Prince of Cats since we were old enough to gain our bonded animals. He's convinced he got the better end of the deal."

"*Ca*," Kieran yelled.

"May I?" Killian asked, extending his arms to his son, who kicked his little feet excitedly.

"Sure, but he's got a *very* wet diaper," Piper warned him.

"Oh, we can take care of that," Killian said.

He moved forward slowly, afraid she would change her mind.

It meant a lot that she would allow him to hold the boy.

Kieran grabbed onto his shoulders and leaned backward slightly to gaze directly into his eyes with a slightly cross-eyed stare.

"Hello, lad," Killian said.

"*Bah*," Kieran replied, bonking him on the nose.

"Let's get you cleaned up," Killian suggested. "There's a stream downhill. We can all bathe."

She nodded and they grabbed their clothing and headed between the trees down to the creek.

It was hard not to stare at Piper's curvy form as she stepped carefully into the cold water, her pretty nipples hardening instantly, sunlight in her hair.

"Well, it's not getting any warmer, is it, son?" Killian asked the boy.

Kieran squeaked at his mother and she waved to him.

Killian managed to undress and bathe the boy without upsetting him too much. The water was cold, but interesting. Again, he could tell how bright the boy was by the way he explored the droplets of water.

By the time Killian had scraped together a bit of magic

to weave a cotton nappie for the child, Piper was finished with her bath and dressed again.

She took the babe, and Killian waded into deeper water.

He bathed as quickly as he could while Piper watched him from where she sat, nursing the baby.

Killian felt happiness he had never known before.

Again, he was tempted to take his little family and disappear. They could live quite happily by this stream for the rest of their lives, as far as he was concerned.

So many thousands of lives will be lost if there is war.

He sighed and waded out of the water, summoning a gust of fall air around himself to dry off.

Piper laughed. "Why didn't you do that for us?" she asked.

"It's cold," he told her, trying not to let his teeth chatter.

"So I guess we keep going now?" she asked, as she lifted Kieran to her shoulder and rubbed the spot between his tender shoulder blades that made him burp like a fire-breathing dragon.

"Yes," he told her, even though everything in his heart cried *no*.

They climbed back up to the spot where they had camped, and she watched as he cleared out every sign they had been there.

"So we can't be tracked?" she asked.

"It's just good manners to leave a site better than you found it," he replied. "The only people trying to track us out here should be members of my own court."

"And what if they're not?" she asked, cuddling the baby closer.

"I will protect you," he told her. "With my life, if necessary."

She arched an eyebrow.

"What?" he asked.

"Oh, nothing," she said. "It's just that last time we were attacked, I believe it was me who saved our asses."

"So then it's my turn next time," he said with a wry smile. "And not all problems can be solved with a bow."

"Sounds like something someone with no bow would say."

She smiled and sunlight burst through the clouds in his heart.

They travelled on for the rest of the day, taking breaks when they needed, and not pushing too hard.

By the evening, he knew they had to be close. The landscape was full of Autumn glory now. The trees shone bright with scarlet and gold.

Piper walked beside him without complaint.

He had always thought of humans as weak creatures, but this one was strong. The baby was heavy, yet she carried him and herself with such dignity, never asking for a break for herself, but only when it was time to feed the child.

"We should be close," he told her quietly.

She nodded, looking thoughtful.

He was about to ask what she was thinking, when the breeze carried a scent to his inner cat.

He snapped his head back to the horizon.

Two figures had appeared in the distance. They were wearing Autumn Court livery. A rescue party, as he'd expected.

Although that wasn't the scent that had caught his attention.

He was probably weary from the journey.

"My men," he said, waving to them. "They'll get us back in no time."

Piper shaded her eyes with her hand.

"How can you tell who they are?" she asked. "They're so far away."

"It's their clothing," he explained, as they walked. "The pale brown leathers with red markings are the Autumn Court livery."

She nodded.

The breeze changed and he scented it again, the same whiff of brimstone he'd thought he tasted before.

"Wait," he told her, putting an arm in front of her.

She froze in place.

He closed his eyes and allowed the lynx closer to the surface.

Instantly, he was drowning in the repugnant scent of some kind of dog.

No. Not just any kind of canine. He knew that scent.

His eyes popped open and he gazed at the horizon in horror.

"Killian?" Piper murmured. "What's wrong?"

"Run," he breathed.

14

———

PIPER

"What is it?" Piper asked, fear creeping into her voice.

What kind of creature could possibly make Killian so upset? He hadn't reacted like this when a giant boar had been charging them.

"A hellhound," he snapped, "Now move."

He grabbed her arm and dragged her back in the direction from which they had come.

Piper ran as fast as her legs would carry her.

But with the baby in her arms, she knew they could not outrun the men and the hound that barreled toward them across the plain.

Killian half-carried her up a rocky ridge.

When they reached the top, she dug her heels in.

"Piper," he panted. "Please. We need to keep moving."

"Wait," she said. "Hold the baby."

He took his son and watched her as she pulled her bow off her back and grabbed an arrow.

"Piper, I don't think that will work," he said.

"Neither will running," she said in a grim voice, her eyes on the plain.

The men and the hound were close enough she could see their faces now. One of the men wore an eyepatch. The other was dressed in dungarees with a suit jacket.

Both were red-faced and panting, wearing furious expressions.

But their anger paled next to the fury of the hellhound.

The beast showed no sign of tiring. Its muscular body seemed built for covering long distances quickly. Sleek fur and muscles stretched and contracted in continuous motion, carrying it closer and closer with each long stride.

Its ears were flat against the broad head that narrowed to a long snout that seemed almost too delicate to house the rows of razor-sharp teeth visible in its horrible smile.

One shot, Piper, she told herself. *Make it count.*

She drew the bow and focused her breathing, slowing her heartbeat before releasing the bolt.

She'd done well with the boar. She could do it again.

She loosed the shot and the arrow sailed out, whistling through the air, deadly in its accuracy. She could tell from the moment it left the bow that it was a perfect shot.

The hound barreled forward as if anxious to meet its death.

Beside her, Killian sucked in a breath, like he knew exactly where the shot was headed as well.

The bolt hit the hound in the center of its chest, the perfect placement to skewer its raging heart.

And it bounced off, careening away harmlessly, like the beast was made of diamond, instead of flesh and blood.

The ghoulish creature shook itself as if it had just taken a pleasant swim, and continued hurtling itself forward at a frantic pace.

"Holy hell," Piper murmured.

"Come on," Killian urged her, grabbing her arm again and taking off.

This time Killian was holding the baby, so she was able to move faster. The child's weight seemed to have no impact on Killian's speed. The huge fae prince was even faster and stronger than he looked. She wondered vaguely if his ability to shift into a lynx had anything to do with it, or if it was some other kind of magic.

Then he was pulling her into the trees, and she had no mental energy to do anything but follow and try not to bash herself into a tree or tangle her feet in the undergrowth.

The forest closed in around them until they could no longer move side by side.

"Go ahead of me," Killian urged her, stepping back.

Piper sprinted on, wondering what he hoped to find that would save them. Surely, they were only prolonging the inevitable. If the beast couldn't be stopped by her bow, and they couldn't outrun it, what hope did they have?

She pressed on, trying to come up with any kind of solution. But she stopped in her tracks when she spotted the man. In the clearing ahead, a tiny patch of sunlight illuminated a figure standing against a tree, waiting. He was huge, even bigger than Killian, wearing the same costume as their assailants.

Piper pulled out her bow and grabbed another arrow, refusing to think about the fact that she was starting to run low. She drew back, hoping that a man wouldn't be able to shrug off her shot the way the hellhound had.

The bow reached full tension and she was releasing the string when Killian grabbed her shoulder.

"Wait," he cried.

Though her fingers had already begun to release, the change of angle caused her to fire off into the woods.

The man leaning on the tree waved.

"That's my brother," Killian said cheerfully.

Piper stared at the big man in front of her in complete shock.

"I almost killed him," she said softly.

"You're not the first woman to have that idea," the man said with a smile as he approached. "I forgive you."

His hearing must be phenomenal to have heard her.

"Heath," he said, offering her his hand.

She offered hers and he grabbed her by the elbow and shook.

"That's a fine bow," he said. "I have never seen its like."

"It's from… the mortal realm," she told him.

It was an odd thing to say about the place she'd called home her whole life. She wondered if it had been a good idea to share that detail.

"You mortals invent the most ingenious things in the absence of magic," Heath said, nodding approvingly

"Thank you," she said uncertainly.

He winced.

"Our kind doesn't care for thanks," Killian said. "It implies a burden, that's all."

That explained Killian's reaction to her thanks earlier.

"Oh," Piper said. "I'm—"

"We don't like that either," Heath interrupted, laughing a deep barrel laugh that told her he wasn't offended.

"Not to break up the party here," Killian said. "But we are running from a hellhound and two men in Autumn Court livery."

Piper turned to see how close their pursuers were.

But there was no sign of the men or the hound.

"They're probably too wise to attack *two* Autumn princes, eh brother?" Heath teased, but there was tension in his voice.

Heath eyed the baby in Killian's arms, but didn't say a word about him.

"Let's get someplace relatively safe," Killian suggested. "And then we can talk all you want."

"My men made camp at an old hunting lodge," Heath said. "It's on a ridge, with a creek below and a cliff behind. No one will bother us without a warning there."

Killian nodded and they followed Heath in silence through the trees. Before long, Piper could see a log cabin on a ridge ahead, a steep cliff face rising behind it.

But a swollen creek blocked them from it.

"How will we get across?" she asked.

"Oh, I'll take care of that, lass," Heath said.

"Great," Killian teased. "You've given him more reason to show off than usual."

Piper turned to Killian, unsure of his meaning. When she turned back, Heath was gone.

In his place stood a massive grizzly bear.

She stepped back instinctively.

"It's him," Killian whispered.

Of course.

"Hop on," Killian said.

She approached the grizzly with caution. But he lowered his snout and gave her a friendly head butt to show he was gentle.

She laughed and allowed Killian to set her astride the beast's broad back.

Under warm fur she could feel thick, reassuring muscle.

Killian handed her the baby and climbed on behind her.

Instantly, the bear waded into the water and began

carrying them across as Kieran squealed with delight and yanked on Piper's hair for emphasis.

She laughed and Killian wrapped his arms around them both.

For a perfect moment she felt the reality of their small family.

For such a long time it had just been Piper and Kieran. Now he had a father around. And a bear for an uncle, for heaven's sake.

Too soon, they reached the other side.

Heath dropped them off at the door to the cabin and then shook himself off, sending droplets flying like a rain storm.

Kieran squeaked happily again, and Piper kissed his soft cheek.

In a heartbeat, the bear was gone, and Heath stood before them once more, only his long, wet hair telling them he was the same creature that had carried them across the swollen creek.

Heath banged a sequence on the door and a man in the same uniform opened it.

"I found them," Heath said gruffly.

Welcoming noises issued from inside and Piper found herself being guided into the dim cabin where a cozy fire crackled in the grate, the delicious scent reminding her of her grandfather's cabin in the Poconos.

Three more men cheerfully rose to greet them.

"Come, sit," Heath told her, leading her to a big chair by the fire while Killian greeted his men. "We'll have a good meal prepared for you soon."

"Tha... I mean, I'm happy to be here," she said, correcting herself before she could thank him.

"It's a pleasure to know you," Heath said politely. "And in

the ruckus, I didn't get a formal introduction. Is this my nephew?"

"Yes, this is Kieran," Piper said softly.

"Hello, nephew," Heath said solemnly.

Kieran observed him wide-eyed for a moment.

"*Bah*," he cried suddenly, and smacked his uncle's cheek, a big smile on his sweet baby face.

Heath tousled the boy's downy hair fondly, then straightened to join his brother and the others.

The warmth from the fire soaked into Piper's tired limbs.

Kieran banged his head on her shoulder, and she lifted her shirt to nurse him, hoping the men wouldn't be embarrassed by it.

For now it sounded like they were staying too busy catching up with each other to even notice her.

Two men were heading out to patrol the borders of the cabin. Two more would go out shortly to hunt some dinner.

Heath and Killian were already scheming about the best way to approach the castle without being set upon by whoever was pursuing them.

"The child is yours, brother," Heath said quietly at one point.

"Aye," Killian agreed. "Wynter asked me to start a child to bring back as our heir. I did not get one on her."

"I knew it," Heath crowed. "I knew she was just hiding in her rooms, pretending."

"Well, you were right," Killian conceded.

"And that's his mother, there?" Heath asked.

"She'll be his wet nurse as far as court is concerned," Killian said. "But, aye, she is."

Heath was silent for a moment.

"Yes, it's as good a plan as can be in bad circumstances," he said at last. "I will do all I can to help her at court."

"Thank you, brother," Killian told him. "She means everything to me."

"That's clear," Heath said softly.

They went back to discussing the merits of various points of entry to the castle.

Piper felt safe and content with Kieran's warm little form curled up against her. When her eyelids grew heavy, she allowed herself to drift slowly to sleep.

15

KILLIAN

Killian paced the plank floor of the little hunting cabin.

Through two watches no one had seen the hound or its keepers. He had to assume someone had called off the hunt.

For now.

And now that the night was fully dark, it was the safest time to move.

"This is the right plan," Heath told him, clamping a hand on his shoulder.

"I know, brother," Killian agreed. "I don't like it, though."

"Which part?" Heath asked.

"I don't like any of it," Killian admitted. "I don't like moving them at night. I don't like her being at court. And I certainly don't like the idea of calling another woman my wife."

"You have choices," Heath said, his voice deep and intense.

"Not when I think of the lives that will be lost if we go to war," Killian said, repeating what he had said so often in his mind. "This is more important than my happiness. There's a generation at stake."

Heath nodded. "Time to saddle up then."

Killian strode over to where his mate curled with their child by the fire.

For a moment he just watched them sleeping. The boy had a chubby fist curled around a handful of his mother's hair, his other hand was splayed out as if he were showing his father how big he was. Piper was smiling slightly in her sleep, arms wrapped snugly around the babe.

"Come love," he whispered to her, stroking her cheek. "We're going now."

She opened her eyes and smiled at him, piercing his heart through with wild love.

He helped her up, and they went outside to where the horses were waiting.

Heath led Killian's favorite horse over. It was a magnificent creature, a dapple-gray draft horse called Wind.

"Hey, boy," Killian murmured to him.

The beast snorted and nudged Killian's belly with his velvet muzzle.

"This is Wind," Killian told Piper. "He can easily carry us all."

It was a shame Kieran was still sleeping on her chest. Killian knew the babe would have loved the big horse.

He lifted Piper on and then hopped up behind her, relishing the feel of her plump bottom against him.

"Ready, brother?' Heath called to him.

"Of course," he called back, wrapping his arms around Piper and taking the reins.

They set off into the night, stars twinkling above.

Though there were men behind and in front, Killian did not like traveling when there was a hellhound about. And of course, there was the whole question of who had sent it in the first place, and what that could mean.

His kingdom was in favor of his marriage to Wynter, as far as he knew. The people were grateful for peace and like it or not, being betrothed to Wynter helped to bring that about.

But the men with the hound had been wearing Autumn livery.

And the hound…

Summoning a hellhound required strong magic.

Which likely meant that someone important was involved.

As they traveled miles into the night he went over and over the faces of the Autumn Court, wondering who would betray him.

At last, they approached the castle from the west, still under the cover of darkness.

The huge stone edifice was more like a mountain than a palace. It half blocked out the moonlight. Flecks of mica in the stone gleamed here and there, and shivering oceans of ivy climbed its walls.

He and Heath had decided it was best to come in through one of the servants' entrances. One of the men dismounted and went to the entry, where the rough-hewn, wooden door creaked open to reveal a dark hallway.

The man waved back to them, signaling that the way was clear.

"Alright, my love," Killian murmured to Piper.

She nodded and stretched a little.

He hopped down and held out his arms to catch her and the baby.

Heath led the way inside with Killian and Piper behind him, as the rest of the men took the horses around to the woods. They would remount and enter the stables from the south.

When Killian's eyes adjusted to the light, he could see that his old nanny Ruthyr was waiting for him, starry-eyed in the kitchens.

"Oh, Killian," she whispered. "Look at your child."

She smiled rapturously at Kieran, earning herself a huge grin from Piper.

"I'll take them from here, love," Ruthyr told him. "She'll see you in the morning."

He froze in place, gaping at her.

But she was exactly right. He was going to have to say good-bye to Piper right here, and watch her leave for the servants' quarters with his son while he went to sleep in his boyhood suite.

"She's the wet nurse," Heath reminded him.

"We'll be just fine, won't we, dear?" Ruthyr said cheerily to Piper.

"Of course we will," Piper agreed. "See you in the morning."

She smiled bravely at him, but he could see the trace of sadness in her eyes.

"See you in the morning," he echoed stupidly.

He watched them wander down the hallway, Ruthyr reaching over to caress the baby's cheek as Piper chatted to her.

It was a happy sight. Piper and Kieran were safe. They would be looked after by Ruthyr, who had a heart as big as Heath's bear.

His scheme had gone exactly as planned.

So why did he feel so hollow inside?

16

PIPER

Piper awoke to the sound of Kieran in the cradle beside her.

She stretched and rolled over, remembering where they were.

Though the walls in the servants' quarters were rough with horsehair plaster, and the single window in the room she shared with her son was incredibly drafty, the whole thing was a thousand times more luxurious than the ground they had slept on during her first night in Faerie.

There were no rampaging wild boars, no stalking hellhounds. In all, Piper felt safe and relaxed.

If someone had told her two days ago that she would feel content waking up in a servant's room in a castle in fairyland she would have laughed like a hyena.

But here she was.

Kieran was sitting on his blanket looked pretty pleased himself. He held a small woolen horse that looked a lot like the big dapple they had traveled on last night.

"Hi buddy," Piper said.

"Ma, ma, ma, ma, ma," Kieran crowed, arms out, fingers wiggling.

She scooped him up and brought him into bed with her to nurse.

A few minutes later there was a knock at the door.

"Come in," Piper called out.

Ruthyr scuttled in with a tray, shutting the door behind her with her generous hip.

"Ah, he's having his breakfast," Ruthyr cried, as if Kieran were the most brilliant baby in the world to have decided to eat breakfast at just that moment.

Kieran popped his head up and gave her a milk-drunk grin.

"No, no, you eat your breakfast, little scamp," she chatted merrily to him as she laid out the tray on the bed. "This is for your mum."

Mum.

Piper's heart froze at the word. No one was supposed to know that. Had she blown her cover already?

"It's okay, love," the older woman assured her. "Your secret's safe with me. I've served master Killian for a long time. I'm not about to betray him now."

Piper relaxed a bit, and her stomach began to growl at the sight of the feast before her. There was an earthenware mug steaming with coffee, a bowl of glistening cut fruit, big hunks of whole grain toast slathered with butter, eggs, bacon, and some sort of pastry, as well as a mug of oatmeal.

But she reached for the pitcher of water first.

"I'll get that, love," Ruthyr said, pouring her out a large glass.

Piper chugged it and felt better instantly.

"Little tykes make you thirsty, don't they?" Ruthyr asked sympathetically.

"Yes," Piper said, grabbing a piece of the heavenly looking toast. She took a bite.

It tasted even better than it looked.

"Want me to keep you company?" Ruthyr asked.

"Yes, please," Piper said. "Unless I'm keeping you from something else."

"Oh, there's always something else," Ruthyr said, waving her hand dismissively. "This is more important. You eat, I'll talk to you about life in the castle."

"This is quite an introduction," Piper said through a mouthful of the most delicious berries she had ever tasted.

"As long as you're the little prince's wet nurse, you'll have a breakfast like this brought to you in bed every morning," Ruthyr told her. "Once he's weaned, if you choose to stay on, you'll have to come down to the kitchen for breakfast like the rest of us."

Piper nodded. That sounded more than fair.

"Of course, this isn't really breakfast," Ruthyr said. "You slept the better part of the day. But I asked cook to make you up a breakfast anyway. Prince Killian said you would like that."

Piper smiled, wondering at the idea that Killian already knew her so well. Then again, who wouldn't enjoy a meal like this?

"The little prince will need more than feeding," Ruthyr went on. "Prince Killian had a word with the staff last night. He insists you're to provide all care for his heir, and that I'm to assist where you deem necessary."

Ruthyr looked worried delivering this news, as if she thought perhaps Piper would not want to be responsible for the baby at all times.

"Oh, how nice," Piper said, kissing the top of Kieran's

head. "That's exactly what I hoped would happen. Don't worry, I won't trouble you often."

Ruthyr nodded once, then fell into silence.

"You'll have to be careful, love," she said at last. "You can't make the truth as obvious to others as it is to me."

"The royal court is dangerous," Piper murmured.

"Oh the royals will take no notice of you," Ruthyr said. "It's the other servants who will be watching. Be careful."

Piper nodded and put down the bowl of fruit. She had suddenly lost her appetite.

"Now you know, so you can mind yourself," Ruthyr said cheerfully, patting her on the knee. "That's all. So is His Majesty ready for the presentation?"

"Oh, I haven't seen him yet today," Piper replied, wondering what Killian was up to.

Ruthyr blinked back at her.

"Oh," Piper realized out loud. "You mean the baby. What presentation?"

She was wondering if she was going to have to start referring to her baby as *His Majesty*, when there was a knock at the door.

Ruthyr hopped up to answer it.

Piper lifted Kieran to her shoulder to burp him, and he banged on her cheerfully with chubby little fists.

"It is time for the heir to be presented before the royal council," a man's voice barked out from the doorway.

A shudder of dread went through her at the thought that they were about to take Kieran from her.

"His Majesty's nurse will attend to him, on the Prince Father's orders," the guard called out.

"I'll have them ready in a jiffy," Ruthyr told him.

Kieran let out a thunderous burp and then laughed.

The door closed.

"Well, the water's not warm, but it's the best we have," Ruthyr said. "You bathe in the tub, I'll wipe down the child. We have suitable clothing for each of you."

Piper handed over Kieran, who chuckled at Ruthyr's smiling face.

She bathed herself as quickly as she could, then looked at the clothing on the bed. There were so many items that it was hard to imagine which went on first.

"Come child, I'll help you," Ruthyr said, placing Kieran down in his cradle. He wore a comfortingly simple white nightgown and bonnet.

After ten solid minutes of fighting with the undergarments, petticoat and dress, Ruthyr stepped back to admire her handiwork.

"Ah, yes, lovely," she said to herself. "Even in this simple getup, your good breeding shows."

If this was considered simple, Piper didn't want to think about the alternatives.

"Uh, thanks," she said, wondering if Ruthyr was complimenting her good posture or her wide hips.

Ruthyr handed her the baby and chased her toward the door.

"Remember," Ruthyr whispered to her breathlessly. "Don't speak unless spoken to, don't argue when Her Majesty takes the child, don't give yourself away."

Piper found herself in the hallway, where the solider who had barked orders in the doorway stood waiting. Kieran clung to her neck, as if he could read her fear.

"This way," the soldier said, taking off so quickly down the long corridor that Piper had to trot to keep up.

The guard, at least, clearly had no idea she was anything more than a wet nurse.

At last they reached a set of double doors, guarded by

two more uniformed men. They threw open the doors at Piper and Kieran's approach, releasing the sounds of great celebration.

Breathe, Piper, just breathe, she reminded herself.

She tottered in the doorway, momentarily astounded by the number of people, the strange food smells, the bright torches.

"Walk to the head of the table," the guard leaned down kindly to tell her. "Let the baby's mother take him, and step back but be ready to retrieve him."

"Th... yes," she said, remembering at the last moment not to thank him. "I will."

She walked as calmly and steadily as she could past the party guests. Though they were dressed more simply at the lower end of the table, the people were all peculiarly beautiful.

The women were delicate of feature and the men were broad shouldered, in spite of their diversity of hair color, complexion and even fashion.

At the head of the table, sat a regal-looking older man, who she assumed must be the king. He didn't seem to be entirely aware of what was going on, but he wore a wide smile, and even at his advanced age, his handsome features were still quite striking. His resemblance to Killian was clear.

She wondered suddenly if Kieran would be blessed with fae good looks.

Piper also spotted Killian's brother, Heath, sitting next to a woman who's cold beauty stood in stark contrast to her kind eyes. Heath didn't offer Piper any acknowledgment, but she'd expected as much, since he wasn't supposed to know her. Still, it was nice to see any friendly faces.

She spotted Killian, who barely spared her an

inscrutable glance before turning back to whisper something to his father.

As Piper approached the head of the table, the room grew quieter, all conversation dimming to a hush of whispers.

Killian stood in a place of honor at his father's side, looking resplendent in green. And beside him a woman in pale blue gown that made Piper wonder how many man-hours were spent getting her into it. She had the perfect, chiseled beauty of an ice sculpture, with less warmth.

Wynter.

The princess gazed so sternly at her that Piper almost forgot to take another step.

She doesn't know. She can't know...

No.

She wasn't paying any attention to Piper at all. She was gazing sternly at Kieran, the way a lioness might consider a gazelle.

Piper felt her heart in her mouth.

I will not hand my son to that woman.

But she had to. If she didn't, he would be in far worse danger. They both would.

Kieran clung to her, as if he could read her mind. To his credit, he did not whimper or cry.

At last Piper reached the woman in the pale blue gown.

The woman looked down her nose at Kieran.

He gazed up at her with big, serious eyes.

Piper felt herself stretching her arms away from her body slightly, offering the child to the woman who would pretend to be his mother. It would have been easier to cut away a part of her own body and hand that over.

The woman wrinkled her nose, making no move to take him.

"I have decided to be more of a hands-off mother," she said almost inaudibly to Piper.

Piper cuddled Kieran closer again, feeling relief, but also a surge of rage at the rejection of her perfect baby.

"Turn around," Killian's deep voice reminded her that he was close. "Let everyone get a look."

Piper turned slowly to face the gathered crowd.

"Lords and Ladies of the Autumn Court," Killian announced loudly. "Princess Wynter and I introduce you to our heir, Prince Kieran."

There was great applause and shouts of the prince's name.

Kieran, for his part, chose this moment to drop his shyness and waved his arms and legs in delight, spluttering a round of congratulatory baby talk in reply, that was heard by no one but Piper because of the din in the room.

"Did the surrogate put up a fight?" Wynter asked Killian quietly.

"She was... surprisingly cooperative," Killian murmured back.

Piper felt a stab of hurt. She knew he didn't mean it, or maybe his words were meant for her to hear, a sort of in-joke.

She kept a silly smile plastered on her face.

"Get them out of here," Wynter sniffed. "I can't eat with that horrible little creature around."

Killian snapped his fingers and the guard who had escorted them in headed over.

"This way, miss," the guard whispered to Piper.

She followed him in a haze, ignoring the faces that leaned closer to peer at the baby. Suddenly, it all seemed like too much, and all Piper wanted to do was get out of there.

At last, they reached the cool air of the passageway.

As she followed the guard back to her room, it was impossible not to mourn the loss of her freedom. In this world, it was clear she was invisible, a pawn and not a player.

Even Killian had just dismissed her without a thought.

Whatever she might have thought was between them, the reality of the situation was that Killian would always put his kingdom first.

And that begged the question - had there really been anything between them in the first place?

Or were his declarations all by design - meant to trick and trap her into cooperating. Convincing her that coming here was good idea was certainly easier than trying to drag her and the baby by force.

And the Fae were known to be tricky.

It's not true. I know he feels what I feel...

But as she arrived in her room with the single window looking out over the frost-laced trees, she found that she wasn't so sure.

17

KILLIAN

Killian watched Piper walk away with their son, his heart breaking with each step she took.

She looked just like any other servant, except for the proud set of her shoulders.

This wasn't the way he wanted to present them at court. This wasn't what he wanted in any way.

Beside him, Wynter picked listlessly at her watercress soup, as if even that flavorless broth offended her somehow.

He closed his eyes and pictured Piper, drawing her bow, biceps flexing, concentration in her eyes like steel.

Nothing was too much for Piper. Not making love to him the night they met, not caring for the child on her own, not protecting and providing for the people she loved.

Piper was all in, all the time. She was fiercely independent, strong, and loyal. And the best he could offer her was the life of a servant - invisible, unimportant, vulnerable to the whims of the court.

He could sneak to her room when his duties allowed, and make love to her furtively, but he could never claim her as his own.

No matter what he told himself she was to him, the truth of the matter was that he'd had to watch her be dismissed from his company tonight and he couldn't lift a finger.

And that was nothing, compared to what might come.

What would happen if he had to watch her be abused, or worse?

Bad things happened at fae court, even the Autumn Court, which considered itself quite civilized.

And *very* bad things happened to humans at a fae court.

It was not just a possibility that he would have to watch her be humiliated or hurt, it was almost certain. And when that happened, he wasn't sure he would be able to restrain himself.

But he would have to, for his people.

I'm going to crack. This mortal girl will break me.

Prince Killian of the Autumn Court couldn't break, or his subjects would be ruined with him.

"Shall we dance?" Wynter asked disinterestedly.

He'd been so lost in his thoughts of Piper, that he hadn't even noticed when they cleared the food away.

Now the smaller tables had been removed to create a dance floor, surrounded by flickering torches.

The players were tuning their instruments, eager to begin. On a night like tonight, with so much to celebrate, they would play for hours, maybe even until dawn.

He would have to start the endless dance, whirling around the hall with a stiff and frozen Wynter in his arms when all he wanted was to run down the corridor like a child and bury his face in Piper's lap so she could tell him it would all be okay.

"Of course," he said, rising to offer the princess his hand.

There was a smattering of polite applause among the

court. Everything they did was applause worthy now. They had presented an heir. The deal was done.

I'm bringing peace to my people, he reminded himself as he led his betrothed to the floor. *This is a victory. This is what I've been working for my whole life.*

But it was a pyrrhic victory.

Wynter placed hands as cold and limp as market fish on his shoulders and he had a quick burst of relief that Piper wasn't here after all, to see him take another woman in his arms.

And the players played on.

18

WYNTER

Wynter approached the horrifying cottage again, Berit and Baird flanking her.

In her hands, she cradled the solution to all her problems.

"Don't just stand there," she said to Berit in a bored way. "Knock on the door."

He scurried forward to comply.

"Come in," the coarse, familiar voice called.

Berit opened the door and held it as she entered.

Wynter stepped inside to find Eyepatch and Suit Jacket sitting at opposite ends of the table, as before.

The hellhound slept on a moth-eaten blanket in the corner of the room, its huge ribcage expanding and contracting with each snore.

"Yer Majesty," Suit Jacket said, without rising.

Eyepatch merely nodded to her.

Icy fury coursed through her, leaving her nearly breathless.

Wynter smiled. It was a cold and beautiful smile, carefully calculated for its effect on men.

"By all means, stay seated," she said. "It's time for us to ruminate on our business so far."

Suit Jacket's eyes widened slightly, and she could sense him consciously trying not to look at the hound in the corner.

"You fucked up," she said crisply.

She wouldn't normally lower herself to such common vulgarity, but it seemed particularly appropriate to the situation at hand.

"You told us not to bump into the other hunting party," Eyepatch said. "But they showed up right away."

"And you dullards chased Prince Killian right into his brother's arms," Wynter said. "As if you were doing it on purpose."

She paused for a moment, pretending to consider.

"Were you doing it on purpose, boys?" she asked "Are you double agents, secretly working for a rival kingdom? Or are you merely so incompetent as to make the options indistinguishable?"

They blinked at her. Or maybe Eyepatch was winking.

In any case, it was clear she wasn't getting an answer.

"And now, since you failed so spectacularly, there's only one solution," she went on. "You will have to kill the baby."

The men exchanged a concerned look.

"It would be a shame to wake the dog," she said lightly, glancing at the beast in the corner and fingering the talisman around her neck. "But I'm ready to do whatever it takes. Are you?"

"Sure," Eyepatch said. "We'll do it."

Wynter dismissed the creature, and it vanished with a puff of smoke and a whiff of brimstone. She kept the charm around her neck. It would be easy enough to summon the beast again if it proved necessary.

"Excellent," she said. "Then I think a toast is in order, to celebrate our new arrangement. Baird?"

Baird scrambled forward with the basket and placed three glasses on the table.

Wynter opened the package she carried. Inside was a bottle of fine, Winter Court wine.

She made a great show of unsealing it and pouring out three glasses.

"Gentlemen," she said, lifting hers. "To finishing what you start."

They echoed her and raised their glasses, but hesitated.

She paused for effect and watched them twist. They'd witnessed her unsealing the wine right in front of them, but they were still afraid to drink before she did.

Maybe they weren't as stupid as they looked. Or acted. Or all accounts so far suggested them to be.

She took a long, slow sip and smacked her lips.

The men relaxed visibly, and both drained their glasses with no appreciation for the fine vintage. Such a waste.

She held her glass out and Baird took it, placing it on the table.

While the men watched, she slid two vials of sticky, amber liquid from her pocket.

She uncorked one and drank the contents without a word.

She placed the other vial on the table as the two men stared at her in confusion.

"I forgot to mention that I need only one of you for this job," she said. "The wine was poisoned with heart of holly. There's one dose of antidote on the table. Whichever of you makes it out of this room will have shown me they have the stomach for the job. Instructions will follow."

She turned on her heel and marched toward the door, Berit and Baird hurrying ahead to open it for her.

By the time it closed behind her, she could already hear the two mercenaries scrabbling for the vial in a fight to the death.

Hopefully, one of them would survive long enough to help her.

And whichever one it was, she didn't think he'd remain seated the next time she entered the room.

19

PIPER

The day after the presentation ceremony, Piper sat with Kieran on a thick brocade blanket in the middle of the palace garden.

When Ruthyr suggested they have a picnic lunch, Piper had had no idea exactly what than entailed.

She looked around at the rose garden, bursting with fragrant fall blossoms, and at the feast spread out before her - enough delicacies for ten people.

If only she and Kieran didn't have to enjoy it alone.

Despite all that had happened, it was hard not to wish Killian were sitting opposite them on the blanket.

Kieran crowed in delight and crawled over to the edge of the blanket to snatch up a flame-colored petal from the lush grass.

"I see that," Piper told him. "You found a flower."

"Mama," he replied, grinning at her and waving the petal around for emphasis.

"Baby," she said. "I love you."

He smiled and moved the petal toward his mouth.

"No, no," she said. "Not in your mouth."

But of course the petal continued on its journey to the little pink lips.

She started to crawl over to snatch it, but movement wasn't easy with so many petticoats and skirts. She wound up tangled in her own garments as Kieran tasted the petal and spit it out, making a horrible face.

"Serves you right, bud," Piper laughed, picking herself up.

Kieran laughed too, and crawled over to her for a cuddle.

"Hello," someone said softly.

Piper looked up to see a lovely young woman in a pale lavender gown. She recognized her from last night's dinner. The woman had been sitting next to Killian's brother. Piper had thought her eyes seemed kind at the time, and was surprised again by the warmth in the regal woman's voice.

"My name is Ashe," she said. "I'm Princess Wynter's sister, which makes me Kieran's aunt."

"It's nice to meet you," Piper said carefully, wondering exactly how much a nanny could talk to a Princess's sister without seeming impudent. "I'm Piper, Kieran's nurse."

"Nice to meet you Piper," Ashe said in a friendly way that made Piper relax just a little.

She looked down wistfully at the meal and the baby.

"Would you, uh, like to join us?" Piper offered. "There's way too much food here. They must think I'm nursing a battalion."

Ashe laughed and seated herself in a fluid motion opposite Piper on the blanket.

Piper wished she had watched more carefully to see how Ashe managed the dress.

"Hello, nephew," Ashe said brightly, but not in a baby talk voice.

Kieran squeaked at her and she laughed.

"You are a very handsome boy," she told him. "I can't wait to see you grow up."

Kieran waggled his fingers at her.

"Oh," Piper said. "That means he wants to go to you."

Ashe opened her arms and Kieran scooted over to investigate his aunt.

When he made it over, he grabbed one of her hands and very slowly pulled himself up to standing.

"Oh, you're showing your aunt your trick," Piper said, pleased.

Kieran pulled himself to standing and sometimes took a few steps while holding onto the coffee table at home. But he wasn't all that interested in walking yet.

Piper's mom always scolded her for holding him too much. But she figured he would walk when he was ready, probably not too long from now.

"Kieran, you're amazing," Ashe breathed.

He grinned at her and then turned back to Piper.

"Mama," he crowed, and lowered himself down to crawl back to her.

"Hi, buddy," Piper said.

"He's wonderful," Ashe said, seeming not to notice that he had called Piper *mama*.

"So, you're from the Winter Court?" Piper asked quickly, hoping to change the subject.

"Yes," Ashe said. "I'm here to see this little fellow presented to the public, then back I go."

"You won't stay to visit with your sister?" Piper asked.

Ashe shook her head, a wry smile on her pretty face. "We're not very close."

Well, that wasn't surprising. It didn't seem like anyone was very close with Wynter. And although the two sisters shared a cold sort of beauty, they couldn't be more different in terms of what was underneath.

Piper was very sure that would be an impudent thing to say, so she kept her mouth shut.

"You're a human, aren't you?" Ashe asked with some interest.

"Yes," Piper said. "I just got here."

"So everything in Faerie is new to you?" Ashe asked. "That must be very exciting."

"I suppose it is," Piper said, nodding. "I'm still trying to get an idea of what it will be like. It's very different here."

"How so?" Ashe leaned forward with great interest.

Piper tried to imagine how to describe the difference.

"In the human realm, we have no kings and queens, at least not in the country, um, kingdom where I live," she explained.

"It sounds dangerous," Ashe said with wide eyes.

"Not really," Piper said.

"But with no one to make laws and enforce order, how do you get along?" Ashe asked.

Oh.

"We have a form of government that allows each citizen to have a vote to decide on leaders who create our laws and enforce them," Piper said. "It's far from perfect, but it seems to work well enough."

"So there is no tribute paid?" Ashe asked.

"You mean like... taxes?" Piper asked.

"A portion of earnings paid to the crown," Ashe said.

"Well, we pay taxes to our government," Piper said. "The leaders we chose use the money to pay for things to help the people. Usually."

"Marvelous," Ashe said. "And who assigns your careers?"

"No one," Piper said. "We choose what we want to do

with our lives."

"Incredible," Ashe said. "How did you decide?"

"I always knew I wanted to be an Olympic archer," Piper said. "So I trained for most of my life. I knew I would need another job as well, but that was the main focus."

"Being a professional archer doesn't pay well in the mortal realm?" Ashe asked in wonder. "Our royal archers are greatly admired and handsomely paid."

Piper suddenly remembered that she wasn't an archer, she was a professional wet-nurse now.

"Well, I had a change of heart, and realized that what I really love is children," Piper said quickly.

"And who could blame you?" Ashe asked, gazing rapturously at Kieran, who was slowly and carefully smearing an entire jar of orange marmalade on his white silk trousers.

"Oh Kieran," Piper exclaimed.

He looked up from his task as if he were surprised, too. Seeing her expression, his little face fell, lower lip trembling.

"It's okay, baby," Piper told him. "I just got distracted talking to your auntie. Let me have that."

He surrendered the nearly empty jar and began sucking on his fingers.

"Well that will keep him busy," Piper said. "Too bad about the mess though, the pants were so cute."

"Can you not remove the jam?" Ashe asked.

"I'll rinse it out when we get back," Piper said.

"Of course," Ashe said. "You are mortal. No magic."

"No magic," Piper agreed.

Ashe leaned in, conspiratorially.

"I don't have magic either," she confided.

Though her voice was cheerful, her eyes were tragic.

"You don't?" Piper asked. She didn't think that was

possible.

Ashe shook her head.

Piper wanted to ask about a million questions. Was it common for a member of the fae royalty to have no powers? Was she respected by the others in spite of the lack? Did she have powers, and then lose them, or was she born that way, just like Piper?

But none of the questions seemed appropriate coming from a servant.

"I'm sorry," Piper said at last. "You're such a lovely person. I'm sure that kindness is a much better trait to possess than magic."

Ashe smiled at her, but it was through eyes hazy with unshed tears. "Thank you, Piper, that was very nice of you to say. I don't even know why I told you about the magic thing. My family doesn't like me to talk about it. It's an embarrassment to them. I guess you and Kieran just put me at ease."

It was a very nice compliment and suddenly Piper felt like against all odds, maybe she was making a friend in the fae realm.

"Thank you," Piper said. "I feel the same. You're the first person here that I feel like I can really talk to."

"It must be so lonely for you," Ashe said. "With no one of your own kind."

Piper opened her mouth to say that she had Kieran, but she was distracted by the sight of a serving boy dashing up.

"There you are," he called to Piper in an irritated way. "It's time for Prince Kieran to be fitted for his gown."

"Oh dear," Piper said. "We're coming."

"It was so nice to meet you," Ashe told her.

"It was good to meet you too," Piper said, lifting her sticky son into her arms and scurrying off after the serving boy who was already hightailing it to the castle.

20

KILLIAN

Killian stood frozen in place for a long time, looking out over the rose garden where Ashe sat alone on the picnic blanket.

Ruthyr had let slip that the nurse had brought Kieran here for a picnic. So Killian had snuck out of the castle like a little boy to surprise her and share a meal together.

But when he arrived, he found her talking with Ashe. And her words had broken his heart.

You're the first person here that I feel like I can really talk to.

He believed her.

Besides Killian, not one member of the court had taken any notice of her at all.

And he had just watched a simple serving boy scold her and send her running to do his bidding.

Meanwhile, she had just told Ashe about the wonders of her own world, how she had been permitted to do anything she liked.

And he had not known that she was a competitive archer before... before he impregnated her and disappeared. Although she'd certainly shown him the fruits of her labor.

He was a monster, no better than the hellhound.

He had chased an innocent woman from a happy life with a bright future into a nightmare where she was held hostage by her love for a child she had not asked for.

And to top it all off, he was sleeping with her, expecting her to sneak around and forgo the comfort of a husband and family of her own so that she could warm his bed when he could be bothered to sneak away.

Waves of sorrow overwhelmed him, and for a horrible moment he wished he had never spotted her through that mirror, never touched her. It had brought unhappiness to them both.

Even baby Kieran would never know a life where his parents could love and be proud of him, together and openly.

So far, Wynter showed no interest in the boy, which was honestly a relief. But when she finally did, he would learn nothing good at her feet.

"I've ruined everything," Killian murmured to himself.

But he couldn't undo it.

They couldn't run away or thousands, of fae would die.

He buried his head in his hands.

There was only one thing in his power to do to ensure her happiness, or at least to ease her misery somewhat.

If he let her go, allowed her to be just the nurse, and not his lover, then perhaps she could find another love. He would find her someone, an honorable man with a comfortable home, and encourage him to court her.

It would hurt Piper not to acknowledge her son as he took his seat at court.

But she could have other children, a home of her own, happiness.

Though Killian knew it would be like knives in his heart

each time he thought of it, her happiness was more important to him than his own.

And all this sneaking around was not honorable. It was beneath her. And it certainly did not suit a Prince of Autumn. He was a man, not a foolish boy. Putting the kingdom's needs first wasn't something he could do by halves. He would pour all the love he felt for Piper into his people. It would have to be enough.

He could just see her figure, tiny in the distance, disappearing into the castle. And even from such a faraway sight, his heart throbbed helplessly, in spite of his good intentions.

21

PIPER

Piper bathed carefully in the cold tub in the corner of her room.

It was late, the sky was black outside the window, and the candlelight gleamed on the surface of the bathwater.

Kieran had fallen asleep quickly tonight after another busy day. And Piper had a feeling Killian would be coming to pay her a visit tonight.

She'd hoped to see him last night, but she heard the party went on until the wee hours. He must have missed her as well, because he'd been trying to catch her eye all through tonight's dinner.

She'd been afraid someone at the feast table would notice.

But they were all too drunk on ale and celebration to make mention of it, if they did. It wasn't as crowded as last night, when she'd presented Kieran and been hustled out. Tonight's dinner had been more intimate, if you could say that about a gathering of twenty people, and she'd been allowed to stay a bit longer with Kieran before he started to get tired, and she excused herself to put him down.

Piper stood and allowed the water to run in rivulets down her body as the candlelight shimmered on her wet flesh.

The door creaked open slowly.

Piper froze.

Killian stood in the doorway, his features soft with wonder.

"Piper," he murmured.

She watched as he barred the door behind him and turned back to her, his big body moving swiftly but gracefully across the space between them.

Her thighs trembled with need at the sight of him.

He lifted her easily from the water and carried her to the bed, laying her down gently, as if she were a child.

"Killian," she whispered, arms open to him.

He pressed his warm body down on hers and though he was fully dressed, she could feel his desire, throbbing hot and stiff against her hip.

She tilted her chin up to kiss him, loving the violent way his tongue sought hers, even as his hand cupped her cheek, so gently.

"Please," she whimpered, clutching at his clothing.

He merely growled and kissed his way down her neck, her breasts, her belly, nudging her thighs apart impatiently.

She didn't have a chance to catch her breath or prepare herself for his frantic assault.

The pleasure was like a tropical storm - sudden, hot, and lush.

She bit her lip until it nearly bled in her effort to stop herself from screaming out her climax when it came.

Killian crawled up beside her and held her close.

Something was wrong. She knew it in her bones.

She buried her face in his chest, clung to him, unable to drag the air into her lungs to ask what had happened.

"We can't go on like this," he whispered.

And just like that, her heart was broken.

"I have a people to answer to," he went on. "A pledge that was made from the moment of my birth. I have to put their interests first. And sneaking around puts everything we've done at risk. If anyone were to find out..."

She was drowning in pain and couldn't speak.

"Do you understand, Piper Lee?" he asked. "Can you see why this is best for Kieran, best for his subjects?"

She pressed her face to his chest. She didn't want to answer. Didn't want to admit that he was right.

"Piper, please." His voice broke on the *please* and she understood that she had no choice.

She lifted her face to look into his eyes.

They were so much like Kieran's. How had she never noticed it before?

She pulled together all the pride and dignity she could muster, drawing it from stores she didn't know she had.

"I understand," she said simply.

It was what he needed to hear.

Tears blurred her eyes.

Somehow, she managed to roll away from his heat and lay back on her pillow.

She closed her eyes and felt him climbing off the bed, heard his footsteps as he walked away, the creak of the door, and the click when it closed behind him.

Then and only then she allowed herself to weep. It was not a pretty cry, with silent tears sliding down her cheeks.

She cried with deep, resounding sobs that made her ribs ache.

The only thing that kept her together at all was her determination not to wake her son.

He will not see me this way. I will be better in the morning.

22

PIPER

Piper awoke early the next morning feeling hollow inside, still reeling from a dream where she had been running through a dark wood, and then suddenly she had just been falling, falling...

But she made a point of taking another quick bath, and tidying up her room.

When the cool morning light slanted through the windows, she made her way to the bassinet and sang Kieran awake.

He smiled his best dimpled smile, and all of a sudden, the ache in her heart lessened and the sun seemed to shine brighter through the windows.

"We don't need anybody else," she crooned. "I've got you, babe."

He seemed to agree.

She rocked him in the wooden rocker while he nursed, his chubby fist locked around a lock of her hair.

By the time Ruthyr appeared with her breakfast, Piper was feeling more like herself again.

"You're up and about early," Ruthyr said approvingly. "Little one need you?"

"I woke up before Kieran," Piper said, shaking her head in wonder.

"He must be resting up for the public presentation this afternoon," Ruthyr said fondly. "Aren't you, Your Majesty? Well your subjects have come from all over the kingdom just to have a look at you, and I don't think they'll be a bit disappointed with what they see."

Kieran decided to sit up at the cheery tone in her voice.

Ruthyr smiled like she had just won a prize, and Kieran grinned back at her, milk-drunk and silly.

"So, my dear," Ruthyr asked Piper, her eyes twinkling. "Have you tried on your gown yet?"

"No," Piper said. "Not yet."

"Well, it's beautiful. And you enjoy it, love," Ruthyr said. "It's the only garment you'll be wearing for some time that is in no danger of his littlest majesty soiling it."

"What do you mean?" Piper asked.

"You get to attend as a guest," Ruthyr said. "The queen will have charge of the wee one."

"I see," Piper murmured, hoping her revulsion at that notion didn't show too clearly on her face.

"Eat your breakfast, dear, before it gets cold," Ruthyr said hopefully, holding her hands out for the baby. "I'll tend to His Majesty for a few minutes."

"Thank you," Piper said, letting Kieran go to her.

"Oh, it's a pleasure," Ruthyr said.

Piper picked at her breakfast as Ruthyr sang to Kieran and sailed around the room with him, pointing out every nook and cranny in the place and showing him the woods out the window.

The sun was high in the sky when there came a knock at the door.

Ruthyr dashed over with a giggling Kieran.

"We're here to take His Majesty for a bath and dressing," a woman's voice said sternly. "The princess wants him to look perfect for the presentation."

"His nurse will accompany him," Ruthyr said, beckoning Piper.

"No," the woman replied. "I'm under strict orders to bring him to his mother. He will return to the nursery this afternoon."

Piper winced at the reference to Princess Wynter being Kieran's mother. She was grateful that Ruthyr was facing the doorway.

Piper gritted her teeth and turned away, so as not to see her son being passed off to yet another woman.

"Well, dearie," Ruthyr said happily, "you've just gotten yourself an hour off. Let's get you into your gown."

There was nothing to do but allow the other woman to help her out of an already elaborate dress, and into the gown.

Ruthyr was right, it was a beautiful thing, made of flame-colored satin that glimmered in sunlight.

But she had already decided the court wouldn't see it.

With all that had happened, she was sure of only two things.

I will never abandon my son.

I will never lose myself to the games of the court.

She might never know whether Killian had only been pretending his feelings for her. It had all been so real to her, but he was a fae prince, bound to the court.

And even if it had been real to him, it hadn't been real

enough to change anything. He'd made that very clear in his visit last night.

So while the others went to drink wine in their finery, and celebrate the induction of her innocent son into the bonds of the court, Piper would wait in solitude, not leaving her room.

"Enchanting," Ruthyr declared as she fastened the last button and stepped away, placing her hands on her round hips in satisfaction.

Piper gazed into the glass and hardly recognized herself.

The woman looking back at her appeared confident and determined in spite of her circumstances. Her eyes flashed with more passion than her fire-colored dress.

The sight of it cheered her slightly and she decided that rather than hiding in her room, she might go for a walk. She wasn't sure where she would go exactly, but it was a big castle. She'd find someplace nice.

"Do you need help with your gown, Ruthyr?" Piper asked politely.

"Oh, no, dearie," Ruthyr said. "But it's kind of you to ask. I'd better dash along and dress. See you at the ceremony."

Piper waited long enough to be sure she would not bump into the older woman in the corridor.

A few minutes later she emerged from her room and jogged down the hallway to the door that led to the gardens, which were the nicest place she'd visited so far.

As soon as she was out of the stuffy castle and under the sunlight, Piper began to really breathe.

She thought about her situation as she walked in the cool air. Pain rushed back into her heart, but so did anger and a mad sort of jealousy.

She stalked toward the rose garden, emotions running wild, safe in the knowledge that every being in the kingdom was gathering back at the castle, ready to watch another woman laying claim to her son and the man she loved.

The weight of it was onerous, and she stopped walking to lean against a maple tree and will herself not to weep.

It didn't work. But at least today the tears ran down her cheeks silently, like in the movies.

"Piper?" The voice was deep and familiar.

"Heath," she turned, surreptitiously trying wipe away her tears.

"Oh, Piper, what's wrong?" he asked.

"He...he doesn't want to see me anymore," she heard herself wail.

Heath moved closer and opened his arms to her.

Mortifyingly, she fell into him and sobbed against his chest.

"That can't be true," he murmured, almost to himself. "My brother can be stubborn, but he's no fool."

"It was all a trick," she moaned. "He never cared about me at all."

"It was most definitely not a trick, lass," Heath said sternly. "My brother is wild about you. He risked everything just to bring you here."

She wanted to believe it, but she had been there, she had heard him say the words, felt the chill of the air on her skin when he had left her bed, taking his warmth away.

"Well whatever he felt, he dumped me," she said.

She was sure those weren't the right words for this place, but he clearly got her meaning.

"And you're going to accept that?" Heath asked in disbelief. "You once tried to shoot me just for being on your path. Yet now you would let your way be blocked so easily?"

Suddenly the world clicked into focus.

He was absolutely right.

Piper Lee didn't let the world happen to her.

Piper Lee took charge and got shit done.

"No," she said firmly. "No, I'm not."

She hitched up her skirts and took off for the castle.

"Wait a minute," he yelled to her. "What are you doing?"

"I don't know," she yelled back. "But whatever it is, I can't do it from here."

KILLIAN

Killian strode down the dark corridor, wishing he could walk away from himself.

He had awoken from dreams of burning, his chest feeling carved out as if from the blades of a thousand knives.

Walking away from Piper was the hardest thing he had ever done. And even knowing it was for her own good, that it gave hope that she might taste happiness one day, he selfishly hated the thought. All he wanted was to wrap himself around her, greedily shutting out the rest of the world so that no one could have any part of her but him.

His court would not look down on him if he did just that - placed her in a cage in the dungeons and toyed with her for decades. She was an outsider, after all, and a mortal, at that.

To openly love and honor a mortal would be blasphemy to his kind.

And he had already given himself to his kingdom.

He stepped into the Hall of Honor, a widening of the main corridor, just before it narrowed again, leading out to the royal balcony where he and Wynter would be holding the public ceremony for Kieran. He could already hear the crowd gathered below.

He spotted Wynter at the threshold of the balcony now, her two serving boys fussing with her gown as the guards looked on, none of them paying a bit of mind to the babe in the pram beside her, in whose honor all of this had been arranged.

He stopped, preferring to commune with the souls in the Hall of Honor until it was time to step onto the balcony and greet his people. The dead made for better company than his wife-to-be.

The walls of the Hall of Honor were covered in paintings of Killian's ancestors. Their battle-scarred armor was displayed on wooden mannequins along either side, and even some of their beautiful old weapons were hung for all to admire. It had all been recently dusted and polished, in preparation for today's event.

He had spent many hours here as a little boy, cheering himself up if he felt sad or lonely by visiting with the Autumn Court of the past and reliving their adventures in his imagination.

Now he looked on the faces with a different eye.

Each and every one of them had made sacrifices to protect their people. Their suffering was made palpable to him now.

There was great-grandfather Aife, his sad eyes gazing back at Killian from the painting. King Aife had allowed himself to be captured as part of an elaborate trick in a war with the Summer Court. Sadly, his chief of war had miscalculated and King Aife wound up dying in a Summer dungeon. But the ruse had worked, and the Autumn Court survived.

Next to Aife was a portrait of Princess Devona, with her bow. The princess had single-handedly protected the court from ruin, balancing on a parapet to take out the leader of a band of raiders with a single shot. Something about her portrait reminded him of Piper and he moved along quickly, passing by her legendary bow, which was displayed in a glass case beside her picture.

But somehow, he couldn't focus on the portrait of Queen Cara. His mind was drawn back to Princess Devona.

Devona had been beloved by their people for her skill and bravery. He had no doubt that Piper would be loved by them too, if only she were allowed to be.

If only they didn't need this delicate peace. And if only he could marry a mortal.

"Prince Killian," a servant's voice interrupted his reverie. "The Princess is waiting."

He sighed and ran a hand through his hair.

I will not betray my kingdom to satisfy my own heart.

I will stand proud for my son today.

I will share this victory of peace with my kingdom.

But it all sounded hollow when he remembered that his true love would be on the lawn below and not on the balcony beside him.

24

___

KILLIAN

Killian walked away from his storied ancestors to join his less illustrious, present-day princess. Somehow, he had a hard time imagining a portrait of Wynter ever making it into the Hall of Honor.

She was currently wrinkling her nose at the baby, who waggled his fingers at her and chuckled.

A small contingent of Killian's personal guards stood nearby, along with a select few officials from his court.

"Kieran," Killian cried to his boy, ready to take him out and give him the cuddle he wanted.

"*Don't*," Princess Wynter said in a tone so commanding he actually took a step backward.

"Why not?" he asked.

"You'll mess up his gown," she said primly. "I'm getting him out right before we go out there."

Out there...

Out there were Killian's people, the fae and other beings of the Autumn Court, all of them relying on him to make a wise choice in his wife, and adoring him for bringing them the promise of continued peace by producing an heir.

He was pondering all this when the large, unfamiliar guard stepped out of his place in line. Which was odd, because Killian made it a point to know all of his personal guards.

Maybe he'd been recently promoted.

It was hard to recognize anyone wearing a full dress uniform and helm, and yet there was still something oddly familiar about the man. He was heavyset, but looked strong, and had a stiff gait, as if he'd been freshly injured. But none of Killian's troops had seen recent battle.

He was about to dismiss his suspicions as nothing more than nervousness, when the man turned slightly, and Killian got a better look at his face.

The sight of the guard's eyepatch instantly transported Killian back to the woods, the trip to the castle with Piper and the baby.

The hellhound.

This guard had been one of its keepers.

The big man moved swiftly across the hall. He reached inside his uniform and withdrew something that shimmered in the sunlight streaming in from the balcony.

Killian looked to his other guards, but they were all focused on Wynter, who was issuing them a strong warning about what would happen if they didn't stand in proper formation during the ceremony.

The imposter headed right for the pram.

At the realization that his son was in danger, Killian's vision tunneled, and everything seemed to move in slow motion.

He screamed and flung himself forward, covering the distance faster than seemed possible. He managed to knock the knife out of the surprised imposter's hand at the last instant, before he could plunge the blade into its intended target.

The man turned to him, an expression of terrified fury on his ugly face.

The imposter threw a quick punch, a wicked hook to the ribs that caught Killian off guard. He tried to roll with it and managed to deflect enough of the blow to keep from having the wind knocked from his lungs.

The man came after him with a wild haymaker after that, but telegraphed it enough that Killian was able to slip under the blow.

He shifted as he ducked, letting his animal form take control. He landed softly on clever paws, and turned to leap back at his attacker before any of the other guards had time to react.

His lynx senses kicked in, and he could smell the acrid sweat beading under the man's armpits as he realized he was outmatched.

He could hear the soft breathing of his babe and he instinctively placed his body between the child and the villain.

The man with the eyepatch glanced over at Wynter, who had retreated onto the balcony, and then back at the baby.

Surely, he would not try to fight a giant lynx to hurt an innocent child.

But Killian read the determination in the man's face before he ever moved a muscle.

As the rest of the guards realized what was going on and began to step forward, the fool in the eyepatch moved for the baby again.

Killian's muscles coiled beneath his fur. He flew through the air, claws unsheathed, and landed on the man's chest.

They hit the stone floor with a sickening crunch that told Killian the man had at least one broken bone.

The air filled with the man's horrible screams.

Killian growled low in his ear and he quieted.

The man inside the lynx battled for control.

Don't kill him, he begged the beast. *We have to find out who sent him. We have to know who wants to hurt the babe.*

The lynx relented and Killian stood into his man form, leaving one foot on the would-be assassin's chest.

A flash of blue light caught his attention.

On the balcony, Wynter's eyes shone madly. She held a ball of writhing blue fire in one hand and clutched that hideous amulet she'd recently begun wearing in the other.

Before his eyes, the fire took shape, splitting into round parts, sliding out into a canine form.

The familiar scent of brimstone filled the air.

"You," Killian breathed, stepping onto the balcony with her. "You sent the men and the hellhound after us."

"Yes, I did," Wynter said without taking her eyes off the fiery transformation happening in the air before her hands. "That's not my baby. And besides, we both know that war is the only solution to our problems."

"You want a war?" Killian asked, unable to fathom her reasoning. "But what about the prophecy? You were supposed to bring peace to our kingdoms."

Wynter only laughed.

"Prophecies are for fools," she spat. "True leaders make their own destiny."

The magic before her continued to grow as she spoke.

"The Winter Court needs a buffer against the encroaching Summer," she said lightly. "Autumn will be cooled to the level of Winter to provide it. When I am finished, Autumn will cease to exist, in all its forms, in order to ensure the survival of Winter."

"You want to *eliminate* an entire season?" Killian asked wonderingly. "That's ludicrous."

"When word gets out that an Autumn guard murdered our heir, then we will have war, whether you want it or not," Wynter continued. "My people will not tolerate it."

"But no one will ever believe you," Killian said. "Maybe if your man had been successful, but there are a dozen witnesses here."

"Someone would have to survive this for word to get out," she said with a wry smile.

The hellhound was almost complete, it hovered an inch from the ground as Killian looked on.

"Seize her," Killian shouted.

Immediately, the rest of his guards sprang into action.

"Oh, I don't think so," Wynter laughed.

The first guard ran for her as the hellhound landed on blue fire paws that turned to solid flesh the instant they touched the stones.

It roared at the guard, and a billow of its wintry breath surrounded the guard like a cloud, freezing him in place.

Killian thought hellhounds dealt in fire, but it made sense, coming from one of Wynter's creations. She perverted everything she touched. Even in the heat of battle, part of him couldn't help but feel relived at the fact that at least now she wouldn't have any part in raising his son.

The beast turned to Killian next.

He prepared his body to shift, but he was frozen before he could even begin the change.

The beast leapt forward, scattering the approaching guards.

"The baby, you stupid mutt, kill the baby," Wynter

hissed. She lifted the talisman over her head to remind the creature who was in control.

Killian begged his body to obey him. He could not watch her kill his child. He would not.

But he was powerless.

Something whistled through the air from behind him, like a streak of dark lightning.

An arrow cleanly pierced the princess's wrist and she dropped the amulet. It tumbled, end over end, before shattering on the stone floor of the balcony.

Killian couldn't see where the arrow came from, but he didn't need to. There was only one person in his court that could have made a shot like that.

Piper.

25

PIPER

Piper was out of ammunition.

She had arrived in the Hall of Honor in time to hear what was happening on the balcony.

As if by a miracle, the glass case next to the painting of the woman in the flame-colored dress had held a bow and exactly one ancient-looking arrow.

And now that shot was used up.

Piper had hoped against hope that the hellhound would disappear again when the amulet shattered.

Instead, it lifted its hideous snout to the heavens and sucked in its first terrible breath of freedom.

"The baby," Wynter screamed at the hound, pointing with her uninjured arm. "*Kill the baby, you worthless beast.*"

Piper sprinted for the pram, lifting the bow over her head like a club. It was carved from sturdy wood, she might be able to fight off the beast for a short time, until help came.

She knew Killian's brother, Heath, couldn't be far behind her. His giant bear might be a match for this wicked beast.

Piper placed herself between the dog and the baby, but

the creature only tilted its head curiously at Wynter, as if trying to understand her words.

"*Now*, you miserable cur," Wynter screamed again, her face twisted with wrath.

But the hellhound was its own master now.

It stalked toward Wynter, frozen breath pluming from its snout.

"No," she said as she backed away toward the railing of the balcony. "*No.*"

But it drew back its lips in a hideous snarl, muscles coiling like a spring, and leapt, snapping its jaw down on her good arm like a bear trap.

Piper watched in horror as Wynter's arm was frozen solid. Tendrils of ice crept from the beast's jaws, up the princess's arm, spreading across her chest, down to her toes, and over her terrified face, until she was completely frozen.

The beast released its grip, and the ice-statue of Wynter toppled over the edge of the balcony.

There was a gasp of alarm from the people gathered below, and then a sound like shattering glass.

Instantly, the hellhound began to smoke and shrink, turning back into blue flame and then winking out.

There was a flurry of movement as the guards unfroze and searched for the man with the eyepatch, who must have slipped away in the confusion.

And there was an uproar among the people gathered in the courtyard just under the balcony.

Piper didn't blame them. It must have been shocking to see your princess killed and learn that the peace being brokered by her betrothal was a sham, all in the span of a few minutes.

She couldn't even imagine the political ramifications that were about to come crashing down on both kingdoms.

But all Piper cared about was Kieran.

She turned and scooped him up, cuddling him close, drinking in his sweet smell, and pledging never to let him out of her arms again. Somehow.

"Piper," Killian groaned, wrapping his arms around her and the baby, though they were in full view of the guards in the balcony and half the kingdom in the courtyard below.

The people began to shout something that made no sense to her.

It sounded almost like a name.

Devona!

"If you tell me there's still another woman to deal with," she said with a smile to Killian as she hugged him close, "I am seriously out of here."

26

KILLIAN

The rest of the day passed in a haze for Killian.

Word was already spreading like wildfire through the kingdom of how the mortal nanny had saved the fate of the Autumn Court, using an ancient bow and a single arrow from the Hall of Honor.

Meanwhile, war between the kingdoms was undeniably afoot, and preparations had to be made. The King had called his sons to his side, and Killian took his place at his father's right hand.

He applied himself to his duty, insisting that Piper and the baby were to be by his side continually, in spite of the shocked expressions of the royal advisors and council each time he put his foot down about it.

Now, as the sun sank behind the scarlet autumn mountains, discussions were winding down and his eyes kept stealing to the rocking chair in the corner where Piper sang softly to their sleepy son.

"Enough," the Autumn King said suddenly, his soft voice commanding. "My eldest has something important to talk to me about. I'll see the rest of you tomorrow."

The lords and chiefs took their leave quickly and scuttled out of the room. Heath gave him an encouraging look on the way out.

Killian stood and waited until the last of them had gone, then turned to his father.

"Be seated, boy," the king said softly.

Instead, Killian knelt at his father's feet.

The Autumn King was stern but fair. All Killian could do was put his happiness at his father's mercy and hope for the best.

"To be a member of the royal family of Autumn is to put the people first," his father said quietly, before Killian could speak at all.

It was a familiar sentiment, oft repeated in Killian's youth whenever he wanted something that was off limits.

"I know, Father," Killian said, his jaw clenched against the desire to beg or storm.

"The young lady comported herself as a royal of Autumn today," the king said with a twinkle in his eye. "It only stands to reason that we make her a member of the family."

Killian's jaw dropped. He looked to Piper, but she was on the other side of the great chamber, out of earshot.

"I mean officially, of course," the king said quickly. "It's clear she is already that to you, and more."

"She is mortal," Killian said slowly, his mind reeling as he tried to catch up to this incredible new reality.

"She is," the king agreed.

"And therefore she cannot be wed to a prince of the Autumn Court," Killian continued, repeating the rules by rote.

"Whose rules do you think those are, boy?" his father

asked. "What's the use in being a king, if I can't use my power for the good of the people?"

"No more rule about mortals," Killian realized.

"No more rule about mortals," the king agreed with a warm smile. "We will have the scribes make the changes and official proclamations it the morning. For now, will you finally introduce me properly to the mother of my grandson?"

But Killian leaned forward to embrace his father first.

The old man hugged him back with surprising strength.

"You should have seen her, Father," Killian whispered proudly to the king. "She was the picture of Devona."

"So I've heard," the old man said with a grin.

Killian straightened and crossed the great room to Piper.

She looked up at him, her eyes radiant, Kieran sleeping on her chest.

"My father wants to speak with you," he told her.

Her eyes widened.

"It's for a happy reason," he said. "Let me take the little one."

She allowed him to scoop Kieran out of her arms and he marveled again at how far they had come in only a few days.

He stayed by her side as she crossed the room to greet his father.

"Your Majesty," she said nicely, dipping into a deep curtsy that was a little antiquated for a modern court, but nonetheless respectful.

The Autumn King gave her a benevolent smile.

"It is a pleasure to meet you, my dear," he said. "You are a brave protector of my grandson."

"It is my honor to serve the Autumn Court," she said at once, warming Killian's heart with her cleverness.

She clearly had no idea what was about to happen. Frankly, Killian was in uncharted territory himself.

"My dear," the king said gently. "I understand you are the child's mother, and dear to the heart of my son."

Piper glanced at Killian, terror in her eyes.

He nodded and gave her a gentle smile.

She turned back to the king.

"Yes, Your Majesty," she said.

"I expect there will be a wedding before long," the king said in a pleased way. "Wartime weddings are simple affairs, but even a simple fae wedding may be luxurious compared to what you are used to."

Piper stood before him. For once, she appeared to be speechless.

"Never mind, my dear," the king said. "I will leave the details to the younger generation. But you will always come to me if you have need, yes?"

"Yes," she echoed. "Yes, Your Majesty."

"That's a good lass," the king said decisively, rising slowly to his feet.

Killian offered his hand, but the old man brushed it aside with a wave of his bony arm.

"See you both at breakfast," the king said, as he exited the room and the guards outside the door fell in behind him.

Killian took Piper's hand and they left together, both of them still too stunned to talk on the long walk through the winding castle corridors.

A few minutes later, Kieran was asleep in the adjoining nursery, and they were alone in Killian's rooms.

"Piper," Killian said softly as he closed the door.

She turned to him, her features soft in the candlelight.

"Everything is different now," she said quietly.

He nodded.

"He accepts us," she said, in a voice that hinted at disbelief.

"You were incredible today," Killian told her.

"I barely remember," she said simply. "All I could think of was Kieran, and you."

The words were heavy with meaning.

"Heath told me what they're saying at the taverns," Killian told her, smiling.

"He did?" she asked.

"Oh yes," Killian told her. "No one can stop talking about the little prince's nanny in the flame-colored gown, taking down the false princess with a single shot from the legendary bow of Devona."

Piper looked down modestly, but not before he saw her delighted smile.

He moved to her quickly, taking her hands.

"I know none of this is what you planned for," he told her. "You didn't expect to be a mother, you didn't ask to be taken to Faerie. You never asked to be a princess, and certainly not the princess of a court at war."

He took a breath and soldiered on. "You didn't ask for me to fall in love with you. But here we are."

She gazed up at him, her eyes luminous.

"Piper, our Kieran isn't preventing a war anymore," Killian made himself say, feeling as though he had swallowed glass. "If you tell me you want to take him back to your own world, I will not stop you. But I will never love another. And if you ever change your mind, I will be right here waiting for you, for as long as I breathe."

"Killian," she whispered.

And then she was going up on her toes, pressing her mouth to his, telling him with her body what she hadn't yet with her words. Promising that she was his. That she would stay.

He pulled her close, until there was no space between them, and devoured her mouth.

They struggled with each other's clothing, grasping at cords and buttons as if they had never dressed or undressed before.

At last Piper stood before him, naked.

Moonlight from the window bathed her in soft light. She was so beautiful that he was afraid his heart might forget how to beat.

He moved to her as if through water. The very air seemed to caress him and slow his movement.

She slid her hands up the planes of his chest, her gentle touch eliciting a violent response from his body.

He fought for control. He had to treat her with reverence, not rut with her madly on the floor.

He took her by the hand and led her to his bed.

She crawled in, maddening him with the movement of her bare hips.

At last she lay in his bed, her hair spread out on the pillows, arms outstretched to him.

Killian had heard the old men's tales, that laying with the same woman grew less sweet with repetition.

But Piper seemed exquisite to him, her beauty more wondrous each time he beheld her.

"Please," she murmured.

He realized he had been standing before her, staring at her as if she were a painting in the Hall of Honor.

He crawled in, pinning her body to the bed with his.

Oh, but she was soft and warm.

He struggled for control as she wrapped her arms around his neck and drew him closer for another delicious kiss.

He kissed her with as much patience as he could muster, soaking in her every sound and tremble.

27

PIPER

Piper felt her whole body go weak as Killian abandoned her mouth to trail kisses down her chest and belly.

His hands were warm and insistent as he nudged her thighs apart, desperate to reach her sex.

She had never been so ready, so frantic for his touch.

For all that forbidden love was supposed to be romantic, this anointed joining was even more so.

Killian tasted her tenderly and she thought she would faint with the pleasure of it.

She closed her eyes and colors swirled behind her eyelids, reds and golds and burnished bronze as his tongue swirled its own pattern against her, sending her closer and closer to paradise.

The teasing ecstasy seemed to go on and on, as if Killian were testing her to see how far he could push her.

When she cried out in frustration, hips trembling with need, he gave her one final lick and then crawled up to cage her head in his arms.

"Are you ready, Piper?" he whispered to her.

She could hear the need in his voice.

"Yes," she whispered.

"This is forever, our joining," he told her. "There is no going back."

"I am yours," she told him.

His eyes went hazy with need.

"And I am yours," he said.

Then he was guiding himself against her, as rigid and impossibly huge as the first time.

She braced herself and was relieved when her body accepted him with only the tiniest stretching pain.

"Piper," he groaned against her neck, threading the fingers of one hand through hers.

He thrust and she thought she would faint with the pleasure of it.

She moved her body in rhythm with his, faster and faster, as if neither of them could get enough.

Killian slid a big hand between them to toy with her.

Piper cried out as the pleasure lifted her out of herself.

She felt him stiffen and jet inside her just as her own climax crushed her back down to him in waves of hot ecstasy.

When the pleasure eased its hold, he rolled them over, pulling her on top of his chest as he panted.

"Killian," she murmured, looking at their hands, threaded together.

Inky black vines had appeared on their skin, twirling around their ring fingers and crawling up to wrap around their wrists, as if they were bound together physically.

"Do you like it?" he asked.

She nodded wordlessly, watching as he separated his hand from hers and they looked down at the markings.

"It means we belong to each other," he told her. "Our fates are entwined. Forever."

She snuggled into his chest and closed her eyes, listening to the beat of his heart.

"Sleep now, my love," he told her.

And this time, she knew he would be there when she awoke.

28

KILLIAN

Killian waited at the edge of the forest as twilight bathed the meadow in sweet pink light.

Kieran rested on his hip, his little face tucked into the crook of his daddy's neck.

The little one was feeling shy, and Killian couldn't blame him. He was feeling more than a bit nervous himself.

After all, he didn't get married to the love of his life every day.

Though it was soon to be wartime, the castle had still gone all out for the ceremony. Magic lanterns led the way from the courtyard to the edge of the forest, their golden flames dancing behind glass.

Flowers had been strewn along the path that would lead Piper to him - camellia blossoms for longing, chrysanthemum for love, crocuses for gladness, edelweiss for devotion, violets for faith and salvia for eternity.

Members of his court stood quietly in the moonlight, each holding a single taper, so that the whole meadow seemed to flicker with candlelight.

The sight was enough to bring tears to his eyes, though all the court was watching.

"Brother," Heath said from his place of honor beside him. "It's lovely, is it not?"

Killian nodded, unable to speak. He felt a rush of longing for Piper, as though she couldn't come soon enough. They had not spent this much time apart since the day she had saved them all.

"She will be here soon," Heath murmured, as if reading his mind. "In the meantime, I need your help."

"With what, brother?" Killian asked, surprised.

"The Autumn Court does not want war. *The daughter of Winter will bring peace to both kingdoms*," he said, quoting the prophecy.

"We already kind of debunked that prophecy," Killian pointed out.

"Did we?" Heath asked. "The Winter Court has more than one daughter."

"Ashe has no magic," Killian pointed out. It was a sad fact that was supposed to be secret. Like most secrets in Faerie, it was known to all.

"She is still a daughter of Winter," Heath said.

"Even if that were true, she wasn't in her room earlier when I sent my men to check on her," Killian said. "I fear she has fled our hospitality."

"I don't blame her," Heath remarked. "Given the circumstances. I should bring her back."

He wasn't wrong. With the looming threat of war, it wasn't a great idea to remain behind what would soon be enemy lines. Lesser courts might choose to exploit that and use her for leverage, even though Killian would never stoop to that.

But if there was any truth to the prophecy...

"How would you even find her?" Killian asked.

"She was spotted near the gates not more than an hour ago," Heath told him. "I have it on good authority that she is headed for the mortal realm."

Killian paused, considering his words.

"Ashe was not involved in her sister's plot," Heath said. "I will find her, and I will marry her. If we can forge that bond, then the Autumn Court will not be torn by war after all."

"But you do not love her," Killian heard himself say.

Heath chuckled.

"It wasn't going to stop you from marrying her sister."

"I feel differently now," Killian said.

"Ashe has always seemed kind," Heath remarked, as if trying to convince himself. "I will find her, and I will try to love her. If you give me your blessing to leave you for a time, that is."

"That blessing is not mine to give," Killian said. "Father is still king."

"He has already given his blessing," Heath said. "I want yours."

Killian turned to gaze into the eyes of his younger brother.

Heath had always been full of merriment, but now his face was solemn. And there was a strange hunger in his eyes.

"Of course you have my blessing," Killian said. "But you must take care. The Winter Court is devious. Promise me you will keep your wits about you."

"Yes, of course," Heath said, looking relieved and a bit more like his jovial self.

Killian wrapped his free arm around him, and the brothers touched foreheads as they had when they were children, as baby Kieran banged a chubby fist on his uncle's chest.

Then the players began their tune, and Heath stepped back so that Killian and Kieran could watch for Piper.

She appeared at the top of the path, swathed in white satin, with flame colored roses in her hair and around her wrists.

She paused, as if waiting for Killian's heart to burst. Then she moved slowly down the petal strewn path, passed the hushed crowd, to join him at the edge of the trees.

"Mama," Kieran cried, breaking the solemn mood.

The crowd tittered as Killian surrendered his son to his betrothed.

Kieran cuddled his mother close and tried to get a better look at the flowers on her head.

"Mama," he said again, trying to use her face as a ladder to reach the blooms.

"Oh, little princeling," Ruthyr cried, handing another well-wisher her taper. "Come see old Ruthyr."

Kieran chuckled and put his arms out to her. Ruthyr always sang to him and showed him the most interesting things around the castle. He already loved her passionately.

Piper surrendered him gratefully, smiling after the two of them as Ruthyr carried the little prince back to her place in the front row of guests.

The words of the ceremony were intricate and lovely, but Killian's mind was too wrapped up in Piper to soak them in.

The stars were twinkling above when he was permitted at last to take her in his arms.

He tucked a hand under her chin, tilting her face so that he could see her beautiful eyes.

"I love you, Piper," he told her. "I will always try to make you happy."

"Too late," she said with a smile. "I'm already always happy when I'm with you."

He kissed her, and the sweet feel of her arms going around his neck as she kissed him back nearly took his breath away.

At last they drew back.

The crowd cheered and the players launched into some upbeat music for dancing.

"I just want to take you to bed," he growled to her.

"Soon, my love," she told him. "But first we dance. Everything is about to change. We might never have another chance to be so carefree."

The Winter Court. His intrepid bride had been a member of the Autumn royalty for less than a minute and she was already thinking about peace negotiations and war.

"Heath is trying to do something about that," he told her quietly.

"Do you think he will succeed?" she asked.

"Yes," Killian said, realizing he meant it. "Yes, I think he will. But I have no reason to believe it."

"You have good instincts," Piper said.

"I spotted you from across the veil between worlds, and every instinct told me to take you," he mused. "I suppose they are pretty good."

She kissed him again and as the crowd cheered in delight, he knew that whatever adventures awaited, they would face them with good spirits.

Together, they could handle anything.

***

Thanks for reading Prince of Cats.
Are you ready to find out what happens when Heath chases

Ashe into the mortal realm, and finds that a dangerous bounty hunter is already hot on her trail?

Then keep reading for a sample of Prince of Bears.

Or grab your copy now!
https://www.tashablack.com/princeofbears.html

PRINCE OF BEARS
(SAMPLE)

1

———

WILLOW

Willow gazed out over her section of the Barry White Diner with satisfaction.

It had been a busy night of waitressing, but all her tables were cleared and reset, ready for the overnight shift to take over.

Willow had a nice little bundle of tips in her pocket, and she was going to be home in time to watch at least half a movie before falling asleep.

She had a couple of murder mysteries and a dance documentary cued up. It was only matter of choosing one, and then heating up a plate of heavenly leftovers from her marathon cooking session yesterday.

These were simple pleasures, but they were all hers.

Willow often wished for adventure, but adventures were hard to come by in small towns like Tarker's Hollow and Rosethorn Valley.

She stuck her head into the kitchen to let everyone know she was headed out.

"See you tomorrow guys," she called to the crew over the sizzle of frying eggs and the hum of the dishwasher.

"You need a ride?" Ramón yelled back. "I'm off in five minutes."

"Nope," she replied. "I got my car back from the shop this morning."

It was nice of him to ask. Her car was old enough to keep her on her toes with needed repairs. Ramón sometimes helped out with a ride after his shift.

"Nice," he said. "So you're on tomorrow?"

"Lunch shift," she told him, rolling her eyes.

"Well, try to get in an early section," he advised. "It's a full moon. Even lunchtime will be crazy."

She nodded.

Say what you would about sleepy little Tarker's Hollow, but the whole town seemed to come to life during the full moon. Even the oldest residents suddenly wanted steak and eggs in the middle of the night when the moon was waxing. And the Barry White Diner was the only twenty-four hour restaurant in the area.

She headed out to her car, glad she wasn't scheduled for the late shift tomorrow.

The night air was cold and crisp. Willow sucked in a deep breath to get the greasy humidity of the diner out of her lungs.

Employees had to park at the back of the lot to leave the best spots for customers. So she was feeling almost fully refreshed by the time she got to her little black compact in the very last spot before the parking lot ended abruptly against a wooded hillside.

She reached for her purse to get her keys, and realized she had left it inside. Again.

Sighing, she turned to head back to the diner. She'd been on her feet all day. Why did another five minutes seem so unbearable?

Sudden movement in her periphery made her turn away from the diner once more. A crash in the underbrush followed.

Something was tumbling down the hillside toward the parking lot and onto the asphalt. No. Not something. Someone.

Instinct made Willow rush to help as a woman landed hard on her hands and knees. A curtain of dark hair covered her face from view. She wore some sort of elaborate gown, as if she had just run away from the Renaissance Faire or a very fancy wedding.

Something about her was familiar.

"Are you okay?" Willow asked, bending to help her.

The woman's face snapped up at the sound of her voice.

Willow stepped back instinctively, feeling dizzy.

The face that gazed back at her was her own.

It wasn't a passing similarity, or a family resemblance.

This woman was her exact double.

Before Willow's eyes, her doppelgänger scrambled to her feet.

"He's right behind me," the woman hissed, eyes wide. "*Run.*"

But Willow was frozen.

She watched her other self gather the gown gracefully in her hands and sprint for the light of the diner that now seemed impossibly far away.

Impossible. This is impossible...

She glanced back to the woods where the woman had come from, to see a man step out of the shadows

He was huge, with wide shoulders, and he wore some sort of costume as well - like a gladiator from that movie with Russell Crowe.

In the cool light of the street lamps, Willow could see the set of his jaw, the fury in his eyes.

Some sort of puppy stood at his feet, hackles raised. It looked more like a wolf cub than any dog she'd even seen.

The man scanned the parking lot until his gaze fell on her. His eyes narrowed as he moved in her direction.

Whatever debt the other woman had been running from, Willow was clearly going to be the one stuck paying it.

2

————

HEATH

Heath curled his fingers around the tiny hourglass that hung around his neck, took a deep breath, and stepped through the veil.

There was a faint rush, like wind in his ears, and the world went blurry, then cleared again.

He was still on a wooded mountaintop, but he knew at once that he was no longer in Faerie. The air here was stale and the darkness incomplete. The light of the nearby city bled all the way to the sky.

Heath had come to the mortal realm with a trifold goal. He closed his eyes and tried to focus.

I will find Princess Ashe.

I will bring her home.

I will convince her to be my wife.

The first two seemed simple enough, but he had no idea how he was going to accomplish that last part. Heath was not in love with Ashe, nor she with him. He had met her exactly twice.

Both times she struck him as overly modest and embarrassed, though kind. She did not comport herself like a princess of the Winter Court at all.

And though it was supposed to be a secret, everyone knew Ashe had no magic to speak of. She was an anomaly, a dud, even in her own eyes, apparently.

He recalled the wording of the fae prophecy that had led him here.

Animosity will grow between Autumn and Winter.

A daughter of Winter will bring peace to both kingdoms.

Heath, along with everyone else, expected that *a daughter of Winter* referred to Ashe's sister, Wynter.

Wynter was as confident and elegant as Ashe was timid and plain. She had been engaged to Heath's older brother, Killian. Everyone hoped that this betrothal between an Autumn prince and a daughter of the Winter Court would seal peace between the two kingdoms.

Everyone except Wynter, that was.

She had secretly plotted against the Autumn Court in an attempt to bring about the every war the rest of them were working to prevent.

And she had gotten herself killed in the process.

So the only daughter of Winter left to bring peace to both kingdoms was the unlikely Princess Ashe.

And now that his older brother, Killian, was marrying a mortal, the only prince of Autumn left to marry Ashe was Heath himself.

Whether she wanted to marry him or not, he was certain she was the kind of princess who would fulfill her duty. At least he had been certain, before she fled to the mortal realm.

Perhaps in time they would grow fond of one another. Heath had always been told that he was a sinfully handsome man.

And Ashe was pretty enough when she wasn't busy worrying about what everyone else thought about her. And more importantly, she seemed like good-hearted girl.

His plan was perfect.

All he had to do was find her.

Poor Ashe had slipped away in the chaos before his brother's wedding. Heath figured she was worried that everyone would suspect her of being involved in her sister's plot.

He didn't blame her. But anyone who had met her two times would know this was impossible.

He scanned the hillside for signs of her passing, but saw nothing that would give him a clue as to her whereabouts.

Though the woodland was sparse compared to the ancient, lush forests of Faerie, it was still thick enough to hide the footsteps of a single princess moving with stealth.

But time was on his side. Ashe would have beaten him here by only an hour or so. She could not have gotten far.

His bear side tugged at his consciousness, asking for control.

There was no reason to deny him.

Heath closed his eyes and shifted into his other form.

Instantly, scents and sounds from miles around slammed into his awareness.

He shook himself, his thick pelt making a satisfying sound that partially muted the others.

He went up on his hind legs and tasted the air, ignoring the thousand mysterious smells that revealed themselves, searching only for the clear, bright scent that Ashe would have trailed along with her from Faerie.

But instead of one trail from his world, he found two.

The first was the pale pink of a frightened runaway.

The other was a blue so bright it seemed to throb.

A bounty hunter...

So Heath wasn't the only one chasing the princess. That complicated matters.

He lowered himself to all four paws and lumbered through the trees as swiftly as he could.

Bare branches reached out to impede him, but his thick fur protected him. He pushed through, slender snout making the way for his big body.

In spite of the circumstances, it was hard not to enjoy himself.

Heath didn't spend as much time in his other form now that he was an adult with responsibilities.

The bear missed running free.

Hurry, he urged it from deep inside. *Someone else is after her too. We have to find her, and we have to find her first.*

Beyond that, there was only so much time in the hourglass. When the sand ran out, Heath would be sucked back to Faerie, whether he had accomplished his goal or not.

The hillside dropped off quickly and the girl's scent grew stronger, as did the trail of her pursuer.

Heath thundered down the precipitous slope until the valley began to reveal itself to him.

He paused to survey the scene below.

Artificial lights illuminated the smooth surface of a lot filled with the human vehicles.

Much to his good fortune, he spotted Princess Ashe right away, and his breath caught in his throat. He slipped back into his human form to explore the unexpected surge of feelings.

The princess walked toward a carriage on the edge of the woods, heading away from a brightly-lit restaurant on the other side of the big lot.

For a moment, he could only watch as he forgot everything - his mission, the other hunter, even his own name - all he could think about was the unmatched beauty of the woman below.

His chest ached, but more with sweetness than with pain.

It was strange. Ashe had always been pretty. But she had never had this effect on him. It was like seeing the sunrise for the first time after a life spent in a dark cave.

She stopped and turned back toward the restaurant, sighing, as if she had forgotten something.

But movement in the underbrush on the edge of the woods caught her attention and she turned back to help a figure that stumbled out of the woods and landed on the hard surface of the lot.

Ice went through Heath's veins as he thought about the bounty hunter. It was a clever trick to pretend to be in distress in order to catch one's quarry.

But before he could take any action he saw it was a woman.

She whispered something to Ashe and then ran for the building Ashe had just come from, skirts hitched up in her hands. Heath wished he'd stayed in his bear form so he would have been able to make out the exchange.

Ashe stood motionless below, looking up into the woods in his direction. Had she sensed him somehow?

More movement near her told him she hadn't been looking at him at all. She'd spotted the bounty hunter.

Instinct took over, and he slipped back into his bear form and charged down the hillside, paws gripping roots and vines, anything that could launch him closer to his goal.

The desire to protect the princess was overwhelming, a deep rooted need that reached far beyond the bonds of obligation and into an abyss of something that felt strange to him.

When he reached the bottom of the hill, he spotted the bounty hunter.

He was fae, tall and broad shouldered with leather armor.

And he didn't see Heath coming until it was too late.

The bear crashed into the big man and sent him sprawling across the paved surface. To his credit, he rolled with the impact, and absorbed most of what could have been a very damaging blow.

The hunter scrambled back to his feet and glared at the huge bear that now stood between him and his quarry. He looked for moment like he was going to challenge Heath for the princess, then he looked from the restaurant to Ashe and back again, and apparently thought better of it.

The man let out a quick whistle and bolted back into the woods, followed by a small wolf cub that Heath hadn't noticed in his haste to protect the princess.

Heath looked back at the woman he'd come to retrieve.

For an instant they gazed at each other, and he had to fight the urge to shift back into the form of a man and sweep her into an embrace.

She did not cower from him, though his bear form was impressive.

Again, he was struck with the maddening feeling that something about her was very different. She was wearing human clothing. Maybe she had been here longer than he suspected.

A commotion from the restaurant drew his attention.

People inside had spotted the bear.

Damn it.

He could not change forms in front of mortal witnesses.

He gazed into the girl's eyes, willing her to follow him, though he had no reason to believe she would.

When he moved around the corner of the building and into the trees again, he was shocked, and pleased, to hear her small footsteps behind him.

3

WILLOW

Against every ounce of her better judgement, Willow followed the bear around the corner and into the forest where he had gone.

She was very sure she was about to be mauled, or worse.

But something compelled her to stay close to the enormous creature, as if he represented the last tenuous hold on her sanity after the unlikely events she'd just witnessed. And he hadn't turned his impressive fury on her. It had almost seemed like he was... protecting her.

She stepped into the shadows, but when her eyes adjusted to the dim light of the woods, she saw there was no bear.

A man stood before her instead, his eyes burning into hers with a passionate intensity. The same look she'd seen in the bear.

It was crazy, but she had no doubt they were one and the same.

The man was tall, with long dark hair, and so beautiful that it made her heart ache.

It was odd to think of such a large man as beautiful, but

there was something tragic about him, something vulnerable in spite of the broad planes of muscle and the strong jaw.

"Ashe," he said, his voice rich with meaning.

She stepped closer, not sure what he meant by *ah-shah.* Maybe it was another language. He certainly didn't seem like a local.

He had just turned from a bear into a person. Could it be bear language?

This is a dream, she told herself. *It has to be. Nothing happening makes sense, not even my own thoughts.*

But when the man lifted a hand to stroke her cheek, she wished ardently that it was real.

His gentle touch sent shockwaves of need through her.

He definitely felt very, very real.

"I found you," he murmured. "I'm going to bring you back to Faerie to take your rightful place."

"Wait, what?" she asked.

"I know why you ran away," he told her earnestly. "But believe me, no one thinks you were involved in that plot. And the Autumn Court will not hold you as a prisoner."

"Plot?" she echoed stupidly, latching onto just one of the many things in his words that made no sense to her.

But he wasn't looking at her anymore. He was staring over her shoulder, his eyes wide.

"He's coming back," he murmured, sweeping an arm around her. "There's no time. We have to go."

His hand was tight on her hip before she could take her next breath.

His other hand wrenched something off from around his neck and dashed it to the ground where it shattered on a rock.

Buffeting wind filled her ears, and her vision blurred.

She opened her mouth to scream, but the sound died in her throat as the world around her slipped away.

She squeezed her eyes shut until the wind died down.

When she opened them again, she was still on a wooded hillside. But there was no mistaking the fact that it was not the same one as before.

The trees were all covered in bright fall leaves. And the hillside sloped down to a meadow with a river flowing through it, instead of a parking lot.

They had not moved, she was sure of it. And yet they had gone. But to where?

A huge, lazy snowflake drifted down, and then another one.

"It's snowing," the man said wonderingly, as if that were the only odd thing going on here.

***

Thanks for reading this sample of Prince of Bears.

Will Willow keep her strange feelings in check long enough to figure out what's going on with her double and the mysterious man who seemed to be hunting her?
Or will the lure of the the handsome man who rescued her and swept her away be too much for her to *bear*? (See what I did there?)

Grab the rest of the story right now to find out!
https://www.tashablack.com/princeofbears.html

TASHA BLACK STARTER LIBRARY

Packed with steamy shifters, mischievous magic, billionaire superheroes, and plenty of HEAT, the Tasha Black Starter Library is the perfect way to dive into Tasha's unique brand of Romance with Bite!

Get your FREE books now at tashablack.com!

ABOUT THE AUTHOR

Tasha Black lives in a big old Victorian in a tiny college town. She loves reading anything she can get her hands on, writing sci fi, paranormal & fantasy romance, and sipping pumpkin spice lattes.

Get all the latest info, and claim your FREE Tasha Black Starter Library at www.TashaBlack.com

Plus you'll get the chance for sneak peeks of upcoming titles and other cool stuff!

Keep in touch...
www.tashablack.com
authortashablack@gmail.com

facebook.com/romancewithbite
twitter.com/romancewithbite